Lucky In Love

Lucky In Love

Jeanne McCann

Writers Club Press
San Jose New York Lincoln Shanghai

Lucky In Love

Writers Club Press
an imprint of iUniverse.com, Inc.

For information address:
iUniverse.com, Inc.
5220 S 16th, Ste. 200
Lincoln, NE 68512
www.iuniverse.com

ISBN: 0-595-16312-2

Printed in the United States of America

Dedication

To my mother, a passionate, emotional woman, who taught her family about love and family loyalty with her life. You always said you wanted to write a romance novel so I wrote one for you. It seems fitting since I learned all I know about love and romance from you.

To my family, who are my biggest critics and my most fierce fans. Heaven forbid, you should ever argue with a member of my family! You will never win.

To my partner, who has put up with the hours of writing and typing to let me fulfill a life long dream.

Thank you.

Acknowledgements

I would like to acknowledge the able editorial assistance provided by Kristin Kirby. It is difficult to review a person's first work with sensitivity. I learned a lot from your advice and suggestions.

CHAPTER 1

Danette jabbed at the intercom button on her telephone. "Cindi, can you come in here for a minute?"

"Be right there."

Danette continued looking at the file in front of her. To an observer, the woman seated at her desk, a beautiful blond wearing a pale crème colored business suit, looked much too young for the title she carried, chief executive officer of the very successful Brennan Company. The firm specialized in providing employment services to other large corporations and was very successful. The office was stylish and elegant matching its occupant, with its large modern desk and conference table. The collection of artwork displayed in the large office was an indication of the owner's interests as it included sculptures, paintings, and many other examples of colorful, creative works.

"What can I do for you?" Cindi's voice interrupted. She was Danette's administrative assistant. Long wavy blond hair, a bright blue knit dress with a silk scarf draped on her shoulders, and a notebook in her hand, Cindi prepared herself to respond to Danette. Not only was Cindi capable of taking shorthand and typing with incredible speed, she also had an incredible knack for organizing and managing the office. She was highly competent at her job, and more than that she was Danette's right hand. She kept Danette's work life organized and controlled, which was exactly what Danette needed in an assistant. Whatever project or job

1

Cindi was given it would be handled with skill and talent and would always meet the project goals. Some people found Cindi to be a little unique. She had four pierced earrings in her right ear and three in her left. She always wore brightly colored clothes, mixing plaids and stripes, and had a tattoo of a parrot on her left ankle. Regardless of what she chose to wear Cindi always managed to look very stylish. She had her very own look. She also had a wonderful sense of humor and was completely loyal to Danette and the company. Denise Johnson, manager of Human Resources, described Cindi as the most talented character she had ever met. Danette and Denise both agreed that she had the most generous heart of anyone they knew. Cindi helped anyone who needed assistance. She was the first to donate to a worthy cause and usually encouraged others to do the same. She was as likable as she was different. Danette considered herself very lucky that she had found and hired Cindi. She was a tremendous asset to the company and one of Danette's closest friends.

"I'm expecting John Booth this afternoon at two o'clock and I don't want to be disturbed. Can you delay my meeting with the finance group until three-thirty?"

"Sure I can, anything else? Do you want me to order lunch in?"

"No, I'll skip lunch today. I've got some paperwork to get through."

"Danette, you are not going to skip lunch again!" Cindi ordered. Danette was a naturally slender person, and she had a bad habit of skipping meals, which at times made her slender frame even more pronounced. Cindi was constantly reminding her to eat. Danette just never thought about food. She had many more important things on her mind.

"Okay, okay, I'll have some yogurt and a cup of coffee, will that make you happy?" Danette rolled her eyes at Cindi. She knew better then to argue with her.

Cindi flashed her a quick grin as she turned to leave. "Yes." Her reply floated back as she shut the office door.

Danette couldn't resist grinning at the closed door. She had met Cindi over eight years ago at a party that Danette had attended. She had been seeing a woman for about two months who lived on Whidbey Island. The woman was, as she put it, madly in love with Danette and had staged a dinner party at her home in order for Danette to meet her friends. Cindi and her girlfriend had been two of those friends. Cindi had introduced herself as Cindi with an I, and her girlfriend, Susan. Two weeks after the dinner party, Danette had stopped seeing the woman and retained the friendship with Cindi and Susan. One year later when Beth, Danette's secretary, had retired after over forty years of service with the company, Danette had hired Cindi. She congratulated herself every day for the smart move.

Beth Livingston had been Danette's Aunt Dorothy's secretary and friend until Dorothy had passed away leaving the company in the capable hands of Danette nine years earlier. When Danette inherited the company she also inherited Beth. Beth had known Danette her whole life and they shared many memories of working with Dorothy. Beth's retirement had left a hole in Danette's small work family and Cindi had filled it with her talent and her personality. Between Cindi and her girlfriend, the only other close friends Danette had were Peter and Michael. Her family was small but very important to her.

Peter and Michael had been lovers and partners for over twenty-five years and Danette had met both of them her first week of college. They remained her closest friends for over twenty years. They had seen Danette through the best and the worst times of her life. In fact, she was going to their home for dinner that evening. She suspected that they were planning a blind date dinner partner for her. They were constantly trying to hook her up with any single woman they considered worthy. They wanted her to live happily ever after and they would do anything in their power to make it happen.

Danette would love to live happily ever after with a woman she just had not found the right one. She was fine when it came to dating but when the subject of living together was brought up Danette panicked. She just hadn't met someone she wanted to share her life with yet. She was fine living by herself.

Danette had met several nice women over the last twenty years but this inability to take the final step was the reason for many a breakup. Several women over the years had pointed out to Danette her weakness in this area. The only true committed relationship she ever had was over twenty years earlier when she lived with Laura Benson. They had met as roommates their first year of college and were each other's first love. It had left its indelible mark on Danette's heart. When her three-year relationship with Laura ended abruptly, she had been devastated. If not for the love and help of her Aunt Dorothy, Michael, and Peter, she would not have gotten through the heartache and gotten on with her life. She did not remember much of her last quarter of college because she had remained in a dazed state for over six months.

Laura had left a month and a half after their three-year anniversary, leaving a note for Danette with very little in the way of an explanation. They never saw each other or spoke again. Danette still had the farewell note tucked away in a drawer. She would never understand why Laura had left and so abruptly. Even after twenty years she still could not even guess what would have made her leave. It would never be something she could accept or forget. As she sat reminiscing, Cindi interrupted her with lunch. Danette welcomed the interruption her memories even after many years were painful.

One hour later, Cindi ushered John Booth into Danette's office and shut the door. Danette had been meeting with John once a month for over twenty years. He was a private investigator Danette had hired. Originally, Danette had wanted to know that Laura was okay, but over the years it had evolved to knowing what she was doing. Danette knew that most people did not understand this need of hers so she kept her activities between John and herself. It was John who told Danette that Laura had married a man twice her age two months after she left

Danette. It was also John who informed her one-year later of the birth of Laura's only child, a girl named Carole. He had provided pictures of Carole as she grew up. Through John, Danette was able to keep in touch with Laura from a distance. She had not told anyone else about her knowledge of Laura. It was enough for her to know that she was okay. It had eased her heart throughout the years to know that Laura seemed happy and healthy.

Laura too, had known grief. Her mother had died eleven years earlier and she lost her husband seven years ago after a lengthy illness. She currently lived at her father's home taking care of him, for over three years earlier he had been struck down by a stroke. She was very active in many charity events, donating her time at a women's clinic and a children's hospital. It was ironic that Laura was doing the very thing she had despised in her mother. Danette could remember Laura making fun of her mother and her charities. It was strange to hear how much Laura had become like her. Beyond her social functions, Laura lived a very quiet life. She had never remarried and there had been no hint of any other relationships.

John interrupted Danette's thoughts as he entered her office. "Good afternoon, Danette, how are you doing?"

"Fine John, how's your wife and children?" Over the twenty plus years their relationship had turned to friendship and they had opened up to each other. Danette knew John was paying for his two boys to attend college. She also had worried with him several years earlier when his wife was diagnosed with breast cancer. She had visited the hospital when John's wife had surgery and had helped John deal with his wife's recovery. John, on the other hand, knew about Danette's relationship with Laura. Over the years, he had developed an understanding as to why Danette needed to know Laura was okay. He somehow knew what Danette needed to hear and provided her with just the right information.

"The wife and kids are fine. Thanks for asking. John Junior is still getting almost straight A's at Western. Jake on the other hand…"

John didn't have to finish his statement. Danette knew all about Jake. She had helped to get him into the University of Washington. Jake was a very intelligent young man who found it hard to apply himself. Partying and causing his parents grief was his current goal in life.

"He'll be okay. He is just finding his way. You wait, he'll work it out."

"I hope so, before he worries my wife and I to death," John responded glumly. The image of the tough private investigator didn't fit John Booth. From the first day Danette hired him she knew he had a heart of gold. He was a large man, about six foot two and two hundred pounds. He was always a little rumpled looking with mussed hair, a wrinkled suit, and a purple and gold Husky tie. His family came first in his life and Danette had great respect for him. He had been a Seattle police officer until his wife expressed her concern at the dangerousness of his job. He quit the force and become a private detective, and his wife had quit her worrying.

"I have some interesting information for you this month. It seems Laura's daughter Carole is going to marry against her grandfather's wishes. Rumor has it that he's threatening to disown her."

"Why would he do that?"

"He doesn't like the boy. It also appears that Laura approves of the match and is helping her daughter and future son-in-law."

"What's he like? Laura wouldn't approve of him unless he was good enough for Carole."

"He's just finished his second year at New York University studying structural engineering and architecture. He is a sharp kid, getting straight A's while working full time. He is twenty-four and has worked very hard to go to college. He had to put himself through school since his parents have several other children to support."

"How did he and Carole meet?"

"At college a year ago. He is from a hard working Italian family from the Bronx. I have a picture of the kid. He's a good-looking guy and, from what I can tell a terrific kid."

"So when are they getting married?"

"It seems that Laura met the family and they are planning a small wedding very soon."

"I wonder why a small wedding, unless Laura's father won't pay for anything."

"I don't think that is the case. It happens that since Laura's husband left everything to her, she is extremely well off and doesn't need father's money."

"So they must want a small wedding."

"Actually, the new son-in-law to be is applying to the University of Washington Architecture department. They have several scholarships available and Carole and her fiancé want to get away from New York. They want to be on their own."

"Why would they come here?"

"From what I can find out it was Laura who suggested Seattle and the University." John paused in his report and looked at Danette. She had listened intently the whole time.

"They want to move here, huh. John, I want you to do several things for me." John took out his pen and opened his notebook to a blank page. He was used to Danette after twenty years. "First, I want you to call Professor Childicotte, he's head of the Engineering Department at the University. Cindi will give you his telephone number. I want you to make arrangements for me to pay for a full scholarship for this young man. What's his name?"

"Anthony Capoletti."

"I want the scholarship to be offered from the University of Washington. He's not to know any different. Make sure it is a full scholarship. Also, tell Professor Childicotte that I will donate twenty-five thousand to the scholarship fund along with payment for this one."

Danette didn't blink an eye as she spoke to John. "Second, I want you to keep me apprised of the wedding. Let me know what happens."

"Will do, Danette." John had never questioned Danette over her vigilance with Laura and her family. He respected her privacy. "Anything else?"

"Not that I can think of."

"Well then, I'm off. I will contact you as soon as I have any more information."

"Thanks John, take care."

"You too, Danette."

It wasn't until John left her office that Danette showed any reaction to John's information. Why would Laura encourage her daughter's boyfriend to apply for a scholarship at the University? Whatever the reason, Danette was gong to help. If Laura's daughter was moving to Seattle, Danette wanted to make it as easy as possible.

"Danette, you have a meeting with the finance group in half an hour. The reports are on your desk." Cindi announced over the intercom.

"Thanks Cindi, I remember."

"Also, you have a five o'clock hair appointment."

"Thanks again, I didn't remember that." Danette smiled. She didn't know what she would do without Cindi. She was invaluable.

CHAPTER 2

Four days later, Danette received a call from John. "Danette, Tony Capoletti has accepted the scholarship and is coming out here next week to find a place to live. Carole is coming with him and she is going to look for a job."

"Good work, John."

"The wedding is August 3rd and then they will drive back out here to get moved in before school starts for Tony in September."

"Okay John. I have some rental homes around the University, let me see which one's available."

"Are you going to rent a place to them?"

"No, I want you to notify Professor Childicotte that one will be made available for them as part of the scholarship." Danette replied.

"That is very generous of you."

"It's not a big deal." Since it was in her power, she would do what ever it took make it convenient for Laura's daughter and her soon to be new husband. There was a reason they were coming to Seattle. Danette wasn't sure what it was, but what ever she had in her power she would use to make it as easy as possible for them.

"Also John, tell the professor that we will provide a job for Carole. When they get here next week she should contact Cindi."

"Okay."

"I want you to handle all the arrangements for the rental home. I will let you know where it is by next week." Danette spoke as she made notes to herself.

"All right Danette. Is there anything else?"

"No, thanks for the good work."

"No problem."

Before she had hung up the telephone, Danette had started a list. She needed to get a lot accomplished in one week.

"Cindi, could you come in here?"

"Sure Danette." Cindi breezed through the door, her outfit catching Danette's immediate attention. She wore a long flowing multi-colored skirt, which swirled as she walked. Along with the skirt she had on a bright blue silk shirt with large sleeves and several silver bracelets on both arms with matching silver dangling earrings. To top it off she had a turban on her head that matched her skirt and a wide black leather belt around her waist with matching black sandals.

"What is this? Are you now a gypsy?" Danette inquired with a grin.

"You like? I thought it added a little mystery to my personality?" Cindi giggled as she twirled in the center of Danette's office.

"It does do that." Danette had to admit. No matter what outlandish outfit Cindi wore, she always looked terrific. She was one of those rare people who could wear anything. "I have a project for you, unless you are going to break out the castanets and dance." Danette just couldn't resist teasing Cindi.

"You should be so lucky," Cindi retorted back with a grin of her own. "What's the project?" She sat down and prepared to take notes.

It was almost a full hour before they were finished and they accomplished quite a lot.

"Danette, do you mind my asking who this couple is?" Cindi inquired, as they were finishing up.

"Laura's daughter and soon to be son-in-law."

"Laura's daughter? Why are they coming here?"

"I'm not quite sure." Cindi was one of only a handful of people who knew about Laura.

"Well, I better get to work then, since we only have one week." Cindi responded.

"Thanks Cindi." She knew Cindi would take care of everything.

True to Danette's plan, Cindi accomplished everything that she and Danette had discussed. A small house by the University was freshly painted and ready for the new tenants, and in one half hour Carole would be interviewing with Cindi for a job. Danette had asked Cindi to interview her with Denise Johnson on the floor below in the Human Resources department. She wasn't ready to see Laura's daughter in person. It wasn't until lunchtime that Cindi and Danette were able to speak.

"She's a pretty talented girl, Danette. You should see her resume. Her grades are almost all straight A's."

"Her mother was very intelligent and talented. She got straight A's when she was attending the University." Danette and Cindi were eating lunch in Danette's office.

"What is her major in college?"

"She was majoring in Business Administration but she isn't going to continue school when they move. She had two years completed, but she is going to support her husband until he graduates, then it's her turn."

"With all of her family money, I'm surprised she has to work at all. You hired her today for what position?" Danette inquired.

"She's going to work for Denise as her administrative assistant."

"Good, Denise has been looking for an assistant for several months. She liked her then?"

"She loved her!" Cindi raved. "Not only does she have terrific office skills, she is very personable, and Danette, she is beautiful."

"So was her mother, Cindi."

"I've never seen a picture of Laura, do you have one?" Cindi asked, curiosity in her voice.

"Yes." Danette's voice had become strained. Opening her bottom drawer, she reached into her purse and pulled out her wallet. She opened it and pulled a photograph from one of the sections. Before she handed the photograph to Cindi she gazed at it. The snapshot was one of both Laura and herself standing in the living room of their rental house twenty years earlier. Peter had taken the photograph one afternoon after they had all gone to the beach. She and Laura were both wearing shorts and tank tops and had their arms around each other. It brought many memories back. The picture was taken at a very happy time. Danette and Laura had been together for a year and a half. For a moment, twenty years fell away. She would never forget how beautiful Laura was. Clearing her throat, Danette handed the photograph to Cindi. Without a word, Cindi took the picture from Danette's hand.

After gazing at the photograph for several moments, Cindi responded. "She does look a lot like her mother. They are both beautiful. You haven't changed a bit yourself, you're just as gorgeous."

Ignoring Cindi's remark, Danette spoke. "What's Carole look like?"

"She has long dark hair, which she had tied back into a French braid. She has green eyes, very large. She is about your height, and she's very slender and graceful. She laughs easily and appears to have a great sense of humor." Cindi seemed to know what Danette wanted to hear. Danette nodded her head as Cindi spoke. "She was very sharply dressed in a business suit, very poised, and articulate. I liked her immediately. Denise likes her too. You would like her."

Danette couldn't respond to Cindi's remarks. She felt to vulnerable at the moment. Cindi handed the photo back to her. Almost absentmindedly, she stared at it, lost in thought. It was several minutes before she put it away. "I wonder if she is as artistic as her mother?"

"Laura painted the pictures in your living room, didn't she?"

"Yes, actually two of them she painted for me. The large one my Aunt Dorothy purchased at Laura's one-woman show. She sold all ten paintings that night. It was very successful. She was going to be famous for her artwork. It was the very next day that she left. No other paintings were ever shown." Danette's voice didn't change expression but her face indicated how painful the memories were.

"They are fantastic, I've never seen anything like them." Cindi had loved the paintings the first time she saw them. They were brilliantly colored flowers and plants intricately woven into wondrous gardens.

"She did have her own unique style." Danette smiled as she remembered Laura and her paintings. It was one of the few things she allowed herself to enjoy, Laura's extraordinary talent.

"Carole's hobbies are refinishing furniture with her husband-to-be, and she hikes and runs."

"I'm glad things worked out. Denise is a good person to work for. Thank you for handling everything. As usual, you did an excellent job."

"Thank you, thank you." Cindi grinned. Danette appreciated Cindi's loyalty. They were not just employer and employee. More importantly, they were trusted friends.

"Danette, do you mind if I ask you a question?" Cindi would not pry if Danette was unwilling to talk.

"Sure." Danette responded.

"Did you ever talk to Laura after she left?"

Danette was caught off guard by the question. "No, I tried calling her and I wrote to her many times. She did not respond. Michael went to New York to talk to her three weeks after she left. She was already engaged and planning to be married within a month, but she did speak to Michael briefly. She explained to him that she had realized that she couldn't stay and hurt me anymore. It would never have worked out. She had made her choice. She told him she loved he and Peter. She also told him to tell me she would always love me." Danette's voice broke as she spoke. She turned away from Cindi as she talked, gazing out the window.

Cindi listened intently. She didn't comment as Danette stopped speaking. Cindi could hear the pain in Danette's voice.

"It is hard to believe that it was over twenty years ago. It still feels like it happened yesterday."

"Danette, how did you know about her daughter?"

"I hired a private investigator who keeps me informed as to how Laura is doing."

Cindi was stunned. "For how long?" Cindi had never known someone who went to such great lengths to keep in touch with an ex-lover.

"For about twenty two years."

Cindi was overwhelmed. "It must have been very painful for you to know what was happening in Laura's life." She couldn't imagine caring that much for someone who didn't love you in return.

"It wasn't painful. I just needed to know she was happy and healthy," Danette remarked "I loved her, I needed to know she was okay."

Cindi again was astounded by the unselfish devotion Danette had shown for years toward Laura. "Is that why you are helping her daughter and her boyfriend?"

Danette shook her head yes. "There is a reason why they are moving to Seattle. I'm not sure what it is, but I will do anything to help Laura's daughter get settled. It's the least I can do."

Cindi had no words to respond with. She and Danette finished their lunch in silence.

After Cindi left her office, Danette's mind wandered back in time to her first day of college in September of 1970. She sat back in her chair as her memories took over.

CHAPTER 3

Glancing around the small half-empty dorm room, Danette couldn't help but feel anxious. She caught her image in the full-length mirror on her closet door and sighed. She looked as nervous as she felt. Her blond hair was uncombed as usual, to the dismay of her fashion conscious aunt. She just never took the time to style it or keep it combed. Her eyes were unusually large as they betrayed her fear. They were sky blue and heavily lashed and, as most people would agree, one of her most endearing features. She was wearing a pair of jeans and a lightweight summer tee shirt, with a pair of well-worn tennis shoes. She grimaced as she noticed that her jeans were loose around her waist. Her nervousness over living in a dormitory was having its usual effect on her appetite. She had always been tall and slender but, as her aunt had pointed out to her that morning, "If I didn't remind you to eat, I swear you would waste away to nothing."

Danette just didn't think about things like eating. She was usually concentrating on something she considered much more important then food. Both of her parents had been taller than average, so her size came quite naturally.

Shaking her already tousled hair, she glanced around the cramped room. There were two small beds, one on each side, with closets and bookshelves surrounding them both. Two desks side by side, another wall with more shelves and storage, and the remaining wall had one large window overlooking the campus grounds. Danette tried to make her side of the room look more lived in by hanging a colorful poster on the wall above her bed, and making it up with bright sheets, blankets, and pillows. It hadn't helped. The room still looked pretty dismal.

She wished her aunt had let her stay at home while she went to college, but she had refused. Living in a dorm room was supposed to help Danette enjoy college, and Aunt Dorothy wanted her to have a chance to learn to fit in with people her own age. Living in a building with two hundred other women, sharing community bathrooms was not Danette's idea of having fun. Going to college was very serious to her and she didn't need any distractions. Her aunt knew how important it was that she do well and had promised Danette if she still wanted to live at home after one year of dorm life, she could.

One full year living in the same room with a stranger frightened Danette beyond belief. She had never had to share her personal space with anyone before and she wasn't sure she could handle it now. Danette had been living with her aunt, Dorothy Sheppard, since her parents were killed in a car accident midway through her eighth grade school year. Her parents had gone out for dinner together one night and, while driving back home were involved in an accident with a drunk driver and killed instantly. Danette's aunt had taken her into her home and heart, and they had nurtured each other back to health. She had taught Danette how to survive her loneliness and go on with her life. There was no one else in their family but the two of them and they were very close. They relied on each other and could talk about anything.

Now Dorothy was making Danette live in a strange room at the University of Washington, not twenty minutes from their downtown condominium, and it made Danette feel abandoned. Her aunt had explained her actions to Danette many times, emphasizing that Danette needed to spend time with people who were her own age. She wanted her to make new friends. Since her parents had died, Danette had put all of her effort into her schoolwork and had dropped out of all social activities, much to the dismay of her aunt. She had graduated with top honors from her high school, earning a full academic scholarship to the University of Washington. She was planning to major in business just like her Aunt Dorothy.

Dorothy had graduated with a business degree from the University some thirty years earlier. She was now a successful wealthy business-woman who ran her own company. She had started out at a young age with a fledgling employment service, and over many years her employ-ment company had grown into a very large, successful corporation. Aunt Dorothy was Danette's only family, and not only did she trust her above anyone, she knew in her heart that Dorothy was doing what she thought was best for her niece. They were each other's lifeline and best friends.

Danette was a shy person and sometimes she found it difficult to develop relationships. Danette's mother and father had encouraged their only child to prepare for college and, since losing them both, Danette had been singularly directed toward that goal, to graduate from college with honors. Danette felt she owed her parents that much and it was her way to show how much she had loved them. Another reason for her all consuming goal, was her desire to follow in her aunt's footsteps. Dorothy's dream was that after Danette graduated from college, she would come to work for Dorothy and eventually take over the business and run it as her own. It was the legacy she could leave her niece and it was a dream they could share together.

Along with her company, Dorothy had accumulated a large amount of commercial real estate around the Seattle area. She could retire at anytime but she loved working. Her employees were treated like members of her extended family and she cared for them as she would her own children. She was active in the civic and artistic communities and was a member of the board of directors for the Opera and the Art Museum. She had sup-ported more than her share of struggling artists over the years. Her love of beauty was shown abundantly in her two-story condominium downtown.

It was full of paintings, drawings, and sculptures of both new and old and some highly successful artists, many of them still on a first name basis with her. Danette had been introduced to and influenced by many of these artists, singers, and musicians, all friends of her aunt's. She had enjoyed every minute of being included as a member of the highly creative, eclectic group of people.

Now here she was going to start college. Her aunt and friends always encouraged her, but moving from home into a dorm room was not a comfortable change. She was going to have to get used to living in a ten by twenty-foot room with two beds and a very public bathroom down the hall. The prospect of living so closely with a stranger scared her to death. She was praying that whoever moved in was neat and easy to live with. Danette was very peculiar about putting things in their place and being organized. Looking at her side of the room, the order of her small space made her feel safe.

Her aunt and a friend had moved her in earlier that morning and it had taken only an hour for her to put her things away. They had taken the time to go pick up her books at the bookstore, and had wandered the campus a bit to get familiar, since classes were starting on Monday. Danette wanted to be prepared and she figured Saturday and Sunday she could get started reading the first few chapters of required reading for her courses. She was going to make sure she got off to a good start. Her aunt had taken her to lunch at one of her favorite places and dropped her back at the dorm suggesting that Danette get out of her room and meet a few of the other girls. She just couldn't get her nerve up to leave the room yet. She wasn't very good at things like that, and she was dreading meeting her roommate even more. All she knew about her was she was from New York State, her name was Laura Benson, and she was due to arrive some time that afternoon. The longer Danette waited, the more nervous she became.

Sitting on a chair in front of her window, Danette looked out across the campus. She was on the third floor and had a sweeping view of the surrounding University. Glancing down at the front entrance to the dorm, she noticed a black Mercedes limousine pulling slowly into the driveway. Opening the window so she could get a better look, Danette watched as the limousine came to a halt at the entrance to the building. Curious as to who would be arriving at the dorm in that fashion, Danette's imagination kicked in. Could it be some politician or celebrity's daughter? The driver's door opened and an elderly gray-haired man stepped out of the car. Walking around to the other side, he opened the passenger door and out stepped a young woman about Danette's age. From Danette's viewpoint, the woman had long dark hair pulled back into a braid. She appeared to be very small and Danette could see a smile on her face. She was wearing dark slacks and a cream colored sweater, very conservative and nothing like the rest of the girls in the dorm.

Danette was still staring down at her not noticing she was hanging out the window, when the young woman looked directly up at her. Danette's breath caught in her throat as, from three floors above, she could see how unusually beautiful the girl was. She had large dark eyes and a full mouth that was curved into a smile, and she appeared to be staring directly at Danette. For several seconds they stared at each other until Danette realized her head and shoulders were stuck completely out the window and she jerked herself back inside. She turned red with embarrassment as she realized how ridiculous she must have looked hanging out of the window staring down at a stranger. Her heart pounded as she sat back in her chair. As she reached over to shut the window she quickly glanced down. She couldn't help but notice the woman was still looking up. Danette's heart was still thumping in her chest as she moved away. She wondered who the woman could be. She obviously was going to the University and living in the dorm. Danette decided to forget about her and get on with her reading.

Grabbing the top book from a large stack on her desk, she burrowed into the corner of her bed stacking pillows behind her. She was prepared to spend the rest of her weekend reading. Whenever her roommate got there it wouldn't make any difference, Danette had made her plans. As she began her first chapter in accounting, the door to her room opened. Danette felt a twinge of nervousness as she prepared to meet her new roommate. She got up off the bed and started for the door as it opened completely. Danette froze as she looked directly into the large brown eyes of the woman who had stepped out of the limousine. She tried to think of something to say, as the woman smiled and walked into the dorm room, several boxes in her arms.

"Hello, my name is Laura Benson. You must be my new roommate, Danette." She smiled as she spoke. Danette couldn't manage to reply, so she just smiled and shook her head. Behind Laura was the elderly man who had driven the limousine. He had two large suitcases in his hands and, as if reading her mind, Laura turned back to the door and spoke to him.

"Richard, I'm sorry, put those suitcases down." He stepped through the door and, nodding his head toward Danette, he placed both suitcases on the other bed.

"I'll go down and get the rest of your things, miss."

"Can I help?" Danette found herself asking, her voice sounding nervous even to her ears. The words just jumped out of her mouth, as her face turned a bright shade of pink.

"Sure, we could use the help, I have a lot more things still in the car." Laura responded with another smile.

Following the two of them down the hall, Danette again noticed how petite Laura was. She must not be more than five feet tall. She made Danette feel awkward. Danette had always been taller then most other girls. Being around small people made Danette very self-conscious about her height.

"I understand you're from Seattle, Danette. Maybe you can show me around. This is the first time I've ever been here." Laura spoke with a smile on her face as she turned toward Danette, slowing her pace to walk with her.

"Sure", Danette managed to reply. "I've lived here all my life. You're from New York, aren't you? What made you come to Seattle?" Danette, still nervous, spoke rapidly.

"It's a long story and to make it short, I came here to study art at the University," Laura responded, as they reached the elevator.

Several more girls joined them and introductions were made. As they rode down the elevator the gentleman named Richard stood in the back silent. When the elevator door opened they all spilled out. The limousine was parked outside the building and had caught the interest of many of the girls by this time. A small crowd had gathered just inside the front door. Marching straight through them, Laura and Richard walked directly to the rear trunk with Danette trailing along. She could hear several of the girls' remarks as they passed.

"I wonder who she is?"

"Can you believe that car?"

"She must be very wealthy."

If Danette could hear them she knew Richard and Laura could, but neither one of them even acknowledged the group of girls gathered or the statements being made. Opening the trunk, Richard pulled out several more boxes and one suitcase. Grabbing the largest box, Richard suggested that they leave the other boxes to him.

"Miss Laura, these things are much too heavy for you girls to carry." At that moment a young man stepped out of the crowd and spoke.

"Hi, can I help carry something?"

Before anyone could answer, he picked up two of the larger boxes, leaving another suitcase and one last box. Danette managed to grab the suitcase and Laura the final box, as the four headed back through the crowd, to the doorway and into the elevator. As they entered, the young man introduced himself as Michael O'Donnell. He was a handsome young man, very athletic looking, with short dark hair, a big wide smile, and was wearing jeans, a sweatshirt, and tennis shoes.

"Hello, I'm Laura and this is Danette and Richard." Laura responded.

"Welcome to the University, girls. Are you both freshmen?"

"Yes."

"What do you do, young man?" Richard questioned, out of the blue.

"I'm a student here, also. I just finished helping my cousin move into her room on the seventh floor. Lucky I came along or you folks would have to make another trip. I'd shake your hand, Richard, but I am temporarily indisposed." He grinned as he looked pointedly at the boxes in his arms.

"I believe I have the same problem," Richard replied with a smile. "Thank you for your assistance."

"Yes, thank you very much." Laura responded.

"No problem. We will have you girls moved in before you know it. What are the two of you taking for classes? Have you chosen a major yet?"

"Business." Danette answered.

"And mine is art."

"Laura, I'll have to introduce you to my roommate, Peter. We are both juniors and he is majoring in art. Maybe I can help you get around the business department, Danette. I'm majoring in Computer Science." Michael chattered on.

"I'd appreciate that."

As the elevator opened, they stepped out and walked down the hall to their room. After unloading the boxes, Michael scribbled his telephone number down and asked for Danette's and Laura's. "I'll have Peter call. Maybe he can help you get settled in your classes. If we can be of any help to either of you, let us know." Smiling, he trotted down the hall.

"He seems like a nice guy," stated Laura.

"You be careful miss, you don't know him. He should be checked out." Richard commented.

"Oh, Richard, you can't check everyone out I'm going to meet. I have good instincts. Don't worry." Laura smiled at him.

"But miss…"

"I know you're worried, Richard, but I'll be fine." She walked over to him wrapped her arms around him and hugged. Richard seemed to be embarrassed by the show of affection but he returned the hug with much enthusiasm. "Now you must get going. I need to get moved in and find my way around," Laura explained quietly.

"Miss, what about dinner, should I come back and pick you up?" He had a worried expression on his face and concern in his voice.

"No, Richard, I want you to go home, you have delivered me safely. " Laura gave him one more hug and a kiss on the cheek. "I am going to miss you very much."

"I'm going to miss you, too. You be careful now." Richard appeared to have tears in his eyes. "I know this is what you want but you call me or the Missus if you need anything. You hear?"

"I promise, Richard, I'll call if anything happens. Now you go. Father will be expecting a report." Hugging him one more time, Laura turned to her boxes and in a muffled voice filled with tears she spoke. "I need to unpack now, thanks for everything."

Danette walked over to her desk and sat down. She felt like an intruder. Richard, taking one more look at Laura, shook his head and started to open the door.

"Nice to meet you miss, good luck in school."

"Thank you." Danette replied. He nodded his head to her and left. Danette started to grab her book again when Laura spoke.

"Richard is having a hard time with my going away to school. He has taken care of me since I was born and he is going to miss me. "

"Is he related to you?" Danette wanted to know.

"He is my dad's chauffeur. He and his wife have taken care of my dad and his home since before I was born. They are like my grandparents. In fact, I wish they were." Laura's voice had become very soft. It was obvious from the expression on her face that she cared for Richard and his wife very much. "Well, I had better get unpacked. Do you have any suggestions on how to store all this junk?"

"As a matter of fact I do." Danette laughed. She had always been a terribly neat person. Organization was her talent.

The rest of the afternoon went by quickly as the two new roommates put things away and talked about school. They both had begun to feel very comfortable with each other. It was like they had known each other for a long time. They chatted all afternoon, never running out of things to say. The telephone interrupted Danette and Laura as they were poring over a map of the campus. Getting to their classes on time Monday morning was their first priority. They both looked at each other with questioning looks. Who would be calling them? They hadn't been in the dorm for a full day. As the telephone rang again, Danette picked it up.

"Hello".

"Is this Laura or Danette?" The voice sounded familiar.

"This is Danette, who's this?"

"Michael, you remember, I helped with the boxes earlier. Are you and Laura settled in yet? My roommate Peter and I want to know if the two of you would like to get a bite to eat. He is anxious to meet a fellow art major."

"Just a minute, let me talk to Laura." Placing her hand over the receiver, Danette spoke to her. "Laura, it's that guy who helped with the boxes today, Michael something. He and his roommate want to take us out for something to eat. Do you want to go?"

"Sure, why not? He seemed to be nice and besides, maybe they can help us find our classes."

Danette took her hand off the receiver. "Sure Michael, sounds like fun. What time and where?"

"Great, how about we pick you up in a half hour. We'll take you to one of the best pizza places in all of Seattle."

"Okay, we'll be ready." Hanging up the receiver, Danette turned to Laura. "They're going to pick us up in a half an hour."

"What are you going to wear?" Laura asked nervously. "I'm not very sure how people around here dress. Where I come from people my age dress pretty formally. I noticed most girls around here are dressed casually. Can you help?"

"Sure," replied Danette with a grin. "That's one thing I know how to do, shop! My aunt thinks it's my only vice. It's too bad you are so tiny; you could wear anything of mine. Let's check out your closet and we'll find something." Danette did have to admit Laura's clothes were a little dressy looking. Grabbing a navy sweater, Danette handed it to Laura. "Why don't you wear this and a pair of jeans?"

"I don't own a pair of jeans." Laura replied with a sheepish look on her face.

"Not one pair?" Danette was stunned. All people their age wore jeans.

"I wasn't allowed to wear them, " Laura replied as she blushed with embarrassment.

"Well, that's all right." Danette responded as she pulled out a sweater from her closet to go with the jeans she already had on. " Just wear the pants you have on. They will look just fine. We'll get you a pair of jeans tomorrow, okay?" She noticed that Laura seemed very nervous and uncomfortable and she wanted to reassure her. For some reason it was important to Danette that she make Laura feel as welcome as possible.

"Terrific," Laura responded with a smile that lit up her face. "I want to make sure I belong. Thanks Danette." With that Laura gave her a quick hug that made Danette blush. It was nice to see Laura smile.

A half-hour later the two of them walked out the front door. Leaning against a beat up old Volkswagen was Michael. Standing next to him was an equally handsome young man with long curly blond hair. He had on a pair of scruffy jeans, bright red tennis shoes, and a paint-splattered sweatshirt. He had a huge smile on his face. Michael raised a hand in greeting.

"Hi ladies, meet Peter. Peter, this is Danette and Laura."

"Hello." He grinned as he shook hands.

"Hi." Danette replied.

"Hello, Michael, nice to meet you, Peter." Laura responded.

"Step into our carriage. It may not look so cute, but it runs." Holding the door open, Peter laughed. Grinning at each other, Laura and Danette climbed in. Michael got behind the steering wheel and off they went. All four began talking at once, immediate friends in the making.

They went to the Northlake Tavern, a famous pizza hangout that all the college students visited, and then off on a tour of the campus. By eleven that evening, they managed to locate all the buildings that Laura and Danette's classes were in. They also took a tour of the Student Union Building, also known as the Hub, the sports complex, and the library.

Laughing and joking all evening, the four of them enjoyed each other enormously. Danette had been a little wary going out with two men they didn't know, especially two handsome men. She did not want to start the year out worried about dating. She had gone out on many dates in high school and in her senior year, Danette had gone out with one boy for several months. He had wanted to get serious but she hadn't felt comfortable with that intense of a relationship. Now she didn't want anything to interfere with her first quarter in college. Peter and Michael seemed perfectly friendly, but not overly, so funny, and very helpful. Danette didn't feel threatened at all and Laura had laughed and giggled all night. They had all teased her about not owning one pair of jeans and she had made Danette promise to take her shopping first thing the next day to get a pair. After promising to meet up with them later that week, Michael and Peter delivered them safely back to their dormitory.

Danette and Laura both crawled into bed laughing and talking about the evening. They had become comfortable being with each other as roommates and had even found themselves finishing each other's sentences as if they knew what each other was thinking. Danette no longer felt alone. She was even looking forward to living in the dormitory, and didn't mind sharing the space with Laura. In fact, she enjoyed her company very much. It was amazing to her that in one short day she and Laura had clicked.

"Danette." Laura's whisper could be heard from across the room. "I'm glad we're roommates."

CHAPTER 4

Time passed quickly as Laura and Danette settled into the routine of college life. They studied, ate, laughed, and grew together in their new-found friendship. The relationship brought a peace and comfort neither had known before. They could talk about everything, and developed a wonderful trust with each other.

Five weeks of classes flew by, as Laura and Danette found themselves seated on their respective beds studying for their first college mid-term exams. They both were taking the first of several on Monday morning. They had studied all week and half the weekend. It was ten-thirty Saturday night, and Danette needed a break.

"How's it going, Laura?" Danette asked from across the room.

"I don't know. The more I look at these paintings the less I seem to remember. Now I know why they told me to get my art history class over as soon as possible. I don't think I have a chance of passing. I feel way over my head." Laura sighed as she put her three-inch thick art history book down.

"I know what you mean. My business economics class is going to be the death of me. I'm getting a headache from all this studying." Danette sat up and stretched as she closed her book.

"Maybe we need a break. How about I give you a backrub and you get some sleep. It's got to look better in the morning."

"It's a deal only if I can return the favor and give you one."

"Okay, but you go first. Lay down flat on the floor on this blanket. In fact, take your pajama shirt off and I'll get some lotion." Laura laid her blanket flat on the floor as Danette slipped out of her top. Even though they had been living side by side for all these weeks, Danette was still very shy when it came to taking her clothes off in front of anyone. Quickly, she dropped on the blanket as Laura approached her with the lotion.

"This lotion is cold. I'll try and warm it up, but I am warning you now." Laura grinned at Danette.

"Okay, go ahead torture me. Besides, I will pay you back, you know. Oh, that is freezing." Danette squealed.

"You're such a baby." Laura laughed as she began to spread lotion on Danette's back with strong smooth strokes. She slowly kneaded her neck and shoulders as Danette started to relax.

"That feels wonderful. My neck feels better already."

"You're awfully tight. Relax and breathe," Laura continued her smooth strokes along Danette's lower back. Danette just lay there enjoying it in total silence, until she almost fell asleep.

"That's enough, Laura. If you don't stop I will fall asleep." Danette sighed reluctantly.

"That's how you're supposed to feel."

"Well, now it's your turn." Danette sat up to put her top back on.

"Okay." Laura grinned as she slipped her pajama top off and laid down flat on the blanket.

"I hope this lotion is still cold." Danette teased, as she squeezed a generous amount on her hands. " I owe you." She laughed as she began to massage Laura's shoulders.

"It's not so bad. I told you, you're just a wimp." Laura giggled as she stretched her arms over her head. "That feels so good. You have great hands, Danette. You could make a living doing this."

"Thanks." Danette blushed as she continued to work on Laura's shoulders. "You're the one who works with her hands."

"Well, whatever you're doing don't stop." Laura stretched out like a cat on the blanket. Danette's stomach fluttered as she watched. She was intrigued with Laura. Everything about her was interesting and kind of sexy. Danette had never known anyone like her. It was such an odd feeling to be drawn to another woman in that way. As she continued to massage Laura's back, she thought about her reaction. Since she really had nothing to compare it to, it must be normal. Other women must feel the same way, too.

"Danette, are you there?" Laura whispered. Danette hands had stilled as she thought about her reactions to Laura.

"I'm here."

"A penny for your thoughts." Laura spoke softly.

"A penny. My thoughts are worth at least a quarter." Danette teased.

"A quarter. They must be pretty serious."

"Nothing that deep, Laura. I was just thinking. Have you ever been in love?"

"No, have you?"

"I don't think so."

"You don't think so. Don't you know?"

"I'm not sure what it feels like. I dated a boy named Rick, my senior year of high school. I liked going out and doing things with him and everything. He seemed to think we were pretty serious, especially when it came to the physical part of the relationship."

"Did you sleep with him?"

"No, I just never thought it was something I was ready for. I'm sure it's one of the reasons Rick and I stopped seeing each other. What about you, did you ever have anyone special?"

"I don't know if I would classify my relationship with Derrick special. Our families are pushing us together. His father and mine are business acquaintances. He is going to Harvard right now. He wants to become a lawyer. We just sort of went to parties and dances together. Actually, Derrick was interested in another girl I went to school with.

She was a real nice girl but his parents didn't approve. So we go out together."

"Are you in love with him?"

"Oh no, he's just like a brother to me."

"Is there someone else?'

"No one. I don't think I have ever felt that attracted to any guy. Maybe I am one of those girls who doesn't come off as sexy. You know, everyone's best friend." Laura chuckled as she spoke.

"Well, I think you're sexy." Danette exclaimed, before she realized what she had said. She blushed with embarrassment over her statement.

"Thank you. Coming from you, I think it's the best compliment I've ever received. You're the one who's so sure of herself. You always look so terrific. I think you're beautiful."

Danette's breath caught in her throat before she could respond. "I've embarrassed you," Laura spoke softly as she sat up.

"No, it's okay. You just surprised me, that's all. Thank you. I value your opinions more than anyone. I'm just surprised you see me that way. I'm not sure of myself at all. In fact, I'm usually scared to death I'll do something wrong."

"That's how I feel most of the time. Maybe everyone feels like that."

"Maybe."

"You know, Danette, I can talk to you about anything," Laura confided.

"I feel the same way. I know you understand how I feel about things."

"I care about you. What you think and feel is important to me."

"You're important to me, too. You're my best friend and I love you."

"I love you too," Laura whispered. She reached over and began hugging Danette tightly. Danette responded by hugging Laura in return. They held each other in silence for several minutes, until Laura pulled away.

"We'd better get some sleep if we are going to pass our midterms." Laura's eyes twinkled as she grinned at Danette.

"Your right." Danette cleared her throat as she spoke. "Goodnight," she said as she stood up to prepare for bed.

"Goodnight, sexy." Laura chuckled. "Sweet dreams." Laura slipped into her bed and turned out the light.

"Laura," Danette whispered in the darkness. "I think you are the most beautiful woman I've ever met."

Laura remained silent for several moments before she responded. "I can't tell you how special that makes me feel. Thank you." The two of them drifted off to sleep.

Weeks later both of them passed their midterms with flying colors and were celebrating their good fortune with Peter and Michael at the Pike Place Market.

"Hey guys, what do you think, crab legs, fresh bread, and a nice big salad for dinner?" Peter inquired.

"Sounds perfect, Peter."

"Okay then, let's grab Michael, finish our shopping, and get out of this crowd. Where is Michael anyway?"

"He's over looking at the jewelry, I'll get him." Laura volunteered as she shimmied through the crowd toward Michael. Peter and Danette watched as Laura linked her arm with Michael and they began threading their way back.

"Aren't they two of the sexiest people you have ever met?" Peter asked as he and Danette watched Laura and Michael stop to laugh at something they saw.

"They both are gorgeous," Danette agreed.

"Well honey, they got us beautiful hunks, so we make some group, don't you think!" Peter and Danette giggled as Laura and Michael arrived.

"Laura told me what's on the menu for dinner, so let's divide and conquer and get out of this zoo!" Michael demanded.

"Okay." Peter agreed. "I'll get the crab legs. Michael, you get the bread. Laura, can you and Danette get the salad stuff?"

"No problem, shall we meet back here?" Laura asked.

"Sounds good. All right troops go do your duty." Michael ordered, a smile on his face.

"Aye aye, captain." Danette saluted as they split up to complete their respective tasks. Within twenty minutes, the four of them were headed out the door toward Peter's infamous Volkswagen, which they named Wilbur. Two and half hours later found all of them sprawled on the floor of Michael and Peter's apartment, recuperating from their meal.

"I couldn't eat another thing!" Danette moaned.

"Either could I," Laura agreed. "But it sure was good."

"That was the best meal I've had in a long time," Michael bragged.

"It was wonderful, wasn't it?" Peter agreed.

"Thanks guys, it's been a great day!" Laura volunteered. "We have so much fun with the two of you."

"That's true. We are so glad we met you," Danette chimed in.

"Are you sure it doesn't bother you that the two of us are gay?" Peter asked, a serious tone to his voice. He and Michael had told Laura and Danette within weeks of meeting them.

The four of them had been out for dinner one evening when a loud group of college boys began to harass the four of them. One of them had called Peter a fag and he had been heartbroken and very angry. They left the restaurant immediately, Danette and Laura very confused and worried about Peter. The trip back to Michael and Peter's apartment was very tense, as Peter remained silent.

"Peter, are you okay?" Laura asked, touching him on the arm as they entered the apartment.

"I'm pissed!"

"Those guys were jerks."

"I know, but it still pisses me off."

"Danette and Laura, we need to tell you something." Michael interrupted. "Peter and I are gay."

Danette wasn't sure how to respond, but she knew she needed to say something. "Guys, we love you. It doesn't matter to us if you are gay."

"A lot of people don't feel the same way." Peter's voice was tinged with sadness. "My parents don't even understand. They kicked me out of the house my senior year in high school."

"You're kidding!" Laura was shocked.

"No. I made my dad sick and all my mom did is cry."

"I'm sorry Peter." Danette hugged him tightly.

"We have been together for a little over three years but we try to keep our relationship quiet. It's easier that way." Michael explained.

Danette remembered that night very clearly. She and Laura had talked about Michael and Peter when they got home. Both of them had agreed that they thought the two of them were perfect for each other. Laura and Danette had promised Michael and Peter they would keep their relationship a secret. It had made them both sad to think that two very special people had to keep their feelings hidden.

"Peter, it doesn't bother either of us that you are gay. We think you both are wonderful. We love you guys." Danette reassured him.

"We love you both just the way you are," Laura added.

"Some people find us hard to take." Michael revealed sadly.

"Not if they met the two of you. You are two of the most generous loving people I have ever met. Tell us how the two of you met?" Danette requested.

"Yes, tell us."

"Well, Peter, do you want to tell them or shall I?" Michael grinned.

"You do it." Peter laughed.

"Well, let's see. I had been in school here at the University a little over a month and was walking through the Quad one morning about nine. I remember the morning clearly." Michael closed his eyes as if to help his memory. "It was raining like mad and I was hurrying to get to my next class. All of a sudden, this blond clod came out of nowhere and knocked me off my feet! Literally," Michael recalled, opening his eyes and glaring at Peter.

"I was late and it wasn't intentional." Peter threw in.

"You mean you really ran into him?" Laura asked laughing.

"I knocked him flat on his back, his books flew one way, and his umbrella another."

"Talk about making a good impression."

"Not only did he flatten me, my chemistry lab notebook was soaked beyond repair. I was also laying in about three inches of water and wet to my skin," Michael reported with a grimace.

"What did you do, Peter?" Laura giggled.

"I apologized several times as I helped him up, then I gave him my telephone number. I told him I would replace the ruined notebook and asked him for his number." Peter sheepishly responded. "I was so embarrassed."

"You were? How about me? My shoes squeaked when I walked and I was completely soaked." Michael reminded him. "And on top of everything else I caught a horrible cold."

"But who took care of you?" Peter questioned with a grin, looking directly at Michael.

"You took care of him when he was sick?"

"Of course! I called him the next evening to offer again to replace his chemistry lab book and he sounded horrible. I volunteered to drop a new one off at his dormitory and he agreed. When I got there he looked and sounded worse than on the telephone. He was running a temperature and sneezing and coughing. I went to the store and got some cough syrup and other stuff. The rest, they say, is history." Peter laughed as he remembered.

"He came over every day to check on me, bringing food and treats for five days. He was so cute." Michael gushed. "Then he invited me out for an apology dinner and we talked all night. We have been together ever since."

"That's so cool. It must have been meant to be." Danette sighed. "That is pretty romantic."

"It sure is," Laura agreed. "You two are lucky to have found each other."

"We are lucky."

"We're just glad we met the two of you. You're our very best friends," Danette added.

"We love you guys, too," Michael responded with a smile.

"Enough of the sweet stuff, let's watch a movie," Peter moaned.

It was several hours later, as Laura and Danette lay in the darkness preparing for sleep, when Laura brought up the subject of Michael and Peter's relationship again. "Danette, does Michael and Peter's relationship bother you?"

"Not at all. I really haven't known any gay couples personally up until now. My aunt has introduced me to some gay people but I never really thought about it before. Actually, I was thinking that they are pretty special the way they love and support each other so much."

"My father would forbid me to be around them if he knew but, I think they are very special. I just hope the two of us are lucky enough to find that kind of love. Wouldn't that be wonderful?" Laura whispered, "You know, Danette, if I was gay, I would look for someone exactly like you."

Danette remained silent for several minutes, unsure of how to respond. "Laura, if I was gay, I would look for someone just like you, too."

"Thanks, Danette." She responded softly. "Goodnight."

"Goodnight, Laura." Danette thought about their conversation quite awhile before she managed to fall asleep.

CHAPTER 5

"Smack." A snowball bounced off the back of Danette as she ran across the front yard of Michael and Peter's apartment building. Laura was chasing her with another snowball. Peter was trying to help Danette, but snowballs thrown by Michael were pelting him. It was a Thursday afternoon, and all four had taken their last final for the quarter. They were celebrating with a free-for-all snowball fight.

Over the past three months, the four of them had become inseparable. Peter and Laura had become kindred spirits with their artwork, Peter with his sculpturing and Laura with her painting, spending many long hours in the art studio. Meanwhile, Danette and Michael spent many evenings studying in the business library and working in the computer lab. Michael was in his third year of business and was maintaining a four point grade average. Danette had been trying to do the very same thing her first quarter of college. Laura and Peter teased them unmercifully about how smart and dedicated they were. All four were singled minded and hard working.

"Whap!" Another snowball bounced off Danette as Laura swooped down on her from behind a car, laughing as she yelled, "Gotcha. What perfect aim."

It was hard to recognize the same girl who had arrived in a limousine three months earlier. She was wearing paint-splattered overalls, high top tennis shoes, and a University of Washington baseball cap, her long brown hair tied back in a French braid. Her cheeks were bright red and her large brown eyes sparkling, from the first day Danette had met Laura, she had flowered. She loved going to college and taking art courses, and her paintings reflected her happiness and sense of belonging. They were large brilliantly colored works containing plants and flowers, a mixture of the real and the imaginary. Her art instructor was so impressed with her talent that he was also encouraging her to show her work. She painted with such passion. Laura was enjoying her college life to the fullest.

Danette was equally as content attending college, but more importantly, she had allowed Laura to become her best friend. She had introduced Laura to her aunt several months earlier, and Dorothy had welcomed Laura into their small family with open arms. Dorothy invited the two of them out many times for dinner, to listen to jazz, or visit with her many artist friends. She had seen some of Laura's paintings and was equally as encouraging. Laura had become a permanent member of Danette's family. They could talk to each other about everything. The other girls in the dormitory teased them because they were so inseparable. Everyone assumed that Laura and Danette were dating Michael and Peter, and it was easier not to explain the truth to anyone. They realized that not everyone was as accepting of Michael and Peter's relationship as they were. Besides, they were too busy to worry about it. Neither Laura nor Danette were interested in dating, chalking it up to their busy schedules. Life for the moment was perfect.

Looking about her through the heavily falling snow, Danette couldn't see Laura or Michael anywhere. Peter was hiding behind his car. "Where did they go, Peter?" She yelled.

"I don't know, but you can bet they have something planned." He replied as he warily stepped from behind the car.

Both of them walked to the entrance of the apartment and they looked around. They could see nothing. As they reached the front steps, the two were pelted with snowballs from above. Looking up, they saw

Michael and Laura leaning out of the second story window of the apartment laughing. Laughing themselves, Danette and Peter ran in the doorway to the elevator. As they walked through the open door of the apartment they were met with more laughter from Michael and Laura. They looked like drowned rats, soaked from head to foot, snow clinging to their clothes.

"Come on, you two, get out of those clothes. You're both soaked!" Laura continued laughing. "You should have seen your faces."

"We'll get you back, you wait!" Danette exclaimed with a smile on her face. "We'll get you when you least expect it. Right, Peter?"

"You bet, but right now I'm cold, wet, and starving? Let's order a pizza. Michael, can you order one while Danette and I change? Come on Danette, I have a tee shirt and sweats you can change into. I'll throw all your stuff in the dryer."

Twenty minutes later all four were huddled in front of the fireplace with blankets, a large pizza on the table behind them. "When are you leaving for Christmas break, Laura?" Michael inquired. "It's been awhile since you've gone home. Are you excited?"

"Not at all. I would rather stay here but my parents are expecting me home for Christmas. I'm to fly out Sunday afternoon." Laura replied. "I haven't been home since school started, so I guess I should go see them. They wouldn't hear of it if I tried to stay here. I did talk them into letting me fly back for New Year's Eve, though."

"What are you doing for Christmas, Danette? Are you going to go stay with your aunt?" Michael continued.

"Yep. Are you guys going anywhere for Christmas Eve? My aunt told me to invite you both to her Christmas Eve party. It is a tradition, and you will have lots of fun, I guarantee it. She always has such an interesting group of people."

"We'd love to stop by. We are going to my parents earlier that evening but we can stop by later," Michael replied.

"Great, she'll like that. I wish you could be here, Laura." Danette remarked quietly.

"I do too, Danette, but my parents are demanding that I come home. Believe me, I'd rather stay here. I just don't want to give my father any reason to pull me out of school. All it would take is for me to anger him and that would be the end of my college days."

"At least your parents want you to visit," Peter remarked quietly.

They all knew that Peter's parents had kicked him out his last year of high school when they found out he was gay. If it weren't for his full scholarship to college and the sale of his sculptures, he would not be able to complete his education. He also missed his family very much. His older sister kept in touch with him but his parents had not spoken to him for over three years. Both Danette and Laura knew how much this affected Peter. No matter how nice Michael's parents were to him, it just wasn't the same. Danette, in particular, knew how lonely Peter felt, because of losing both of her parents several years earlier. She still missed them especially during the holidays.

"Laura, you said you are going to be back for New Years Eve?" Peter asked. "Michael and I are going to a great New Year's Eve party. Would you and Danette like to go with us to the party? We can celebrate the New Year with our best friends. What could be better? Besides, it's on a boat that cruises around Lake Washington and there's food and dancing. There will probably be mostly gay people there, but it should be great fun. What do you say?"

"I fly in New Year's Eve afternoon, so I'll be here. I would love to go to the party if Danette wants to. What do you think?" Laura asked Danette.

"I'm game. I can pick you up at the airport. We can stay at my Aunt's if you want to and go to the party from there." Danette grinned. "It sounds like a blast!"

"We'll pick you up there. It'll be great!" Michael stated," We'll have a great time—the four Musketeers ride again!" They all laughed.

Two days later, Danette and Laura were standing at the airport gate waiting for Laura's flight back to New York. It would be boarding any moment. Neither one had wanted to exchange Christmas gifts until Laura came back from New York. They were going to miss each other very much, but would have something to look forward to. Earlier that day Michael and Peter had stopped over to say their goodbyes.

"We are now boarding flight six fifty-four to New York City," the voice stated over the intercom.

"That's my flight," Laura said softly. "I've got to go, I'm going to miss you." Laura threw her arms around Danette.

"I'm going to miss you, too," Danette whispered back, hugging her tightly. "Be careful and call me if you get lonely."

"I will," Laura responded. Before Danette could say another word Laura kissed her quickly on the cheek and pulled away. Danette could feel her eyes welling up with tears and her fingertips touched her cheek where Laura's lips had kissed her. She watched as Laura walked through the gate and, at the last minute, turned and waved. Danette raised her hand to wave back. The last image she had of Laura was the back of her with her long brown hair pulled back into a single braid. She was not in her usual jeans and tennis shoes, but had an outfit on exactly like the one she had been wearing the very first day Danette saw her stepping out of the limousine.

Danette turned away from the gate and started for home. She already missed Laura. That evening she decided to stay at the dormitory before moving back to her aunt's place for a week. Even though Laura was gone, it made Danette feel a little less lonely staying in their room for the night. She was finding it hard to sleep, as she tossed and turned, when the telephone rang.

"Hello."

"Danette, its Laura."

"Laura, what time is it back there?"

"It's after three in the morning. I'm sorry I woke you up."

"That's okay, is everything all right?"

"Everything's fine. Mother and Father had Derrick pick me up at the airport. I guess they still think we are a couple. They have planned a formal welcome home party for me tonight and have invited quite a lot of people."

"Sounds fun," Danette responded, trying to sound excited. She actually felt a little sick inside and could not figure out why.

"Danette, you sound funny."

"I'm just not awake, I'm fine." Danette tried to reassure her but even her own voice didn't sound too convincing.

"Well, I won't keep you up." Laura's voice sounded hurt. "I just called to let you know I arrived safely and I miss you."

"I'm glad you're there in one piece and I miss you too. Enjoy your party." Danette tried very hard to sound happy.

"I'll call you later this week. Will you be at your Aunt's?"

"Yes, I'm going over there tomorrow morning."

"Take care, Danette."

"You too, Laura. I'm glad you called." As Danette placed the telephone receiver down she felt like crying. She didn't understand why, she just felt sad through and through. Sleep was long in coming as she lay there for several hours trying to understand her feelings.

Laura, many miles away, was equally as dismal. Laura missed Danette badly and had needed to know she felt the same way. Danette had not sounded like she missed her in the least. Laura's heart hurt as she tried to sleep. She had no idea why she felt so bad.

Danette spent two full days in misery, working at her aunt's company. It wasn't the work that bothered her. She knew it had everything to do with Laura. When Laura hadn't called by late Tuesday evening, Danette was beside herself. She finally crawled into bed at eleven; heartbroken that Laura didn't seem to want to talk to her. She obviously had more important things to do. The more Danette tried to ignore her feelings the worse they got. She couldn't figure out why the idea of Laura having a good time with Derrick was so disturbing. It was almost as if she was jealous, but that couldn't be the case. Tossing and turning, Danette could not find any relief.

Laura was miserable at the party. Not only did her parents intimate to everyone that she and Derrick were all but engaged to be married, they had tried to announce that very fact at the party. It had taken Derrick and Laura several minutes of talking to convince both sets of parents that they were not going to marry each other.

"Derrick, what's wrong with my parents?"

"Laura, they live in a very old fashioned, old money world. Arranged marriages are normal to them." Derrick hugged his good friend. "They have no idea what it is like to marry someone because of love."

"Don't you want that?"

"Of course I do. I just need to make sure that I don't totally piss my parents off before I graduate from Harvard. I can't afford to pay for college and I need the degree to get into law school."

"I don't know if I can take much more of my father. He is so close to demanding that I come home. I just can't Derrick." Laura sounded almost panicked.

"Honey, what is the worst that would happen? If you really want to stay in school it shouldn't matter what your father does. You could get a loan."

"Derrick, Father scares me."

"Laura honey, he is your father, not some monster. What does your mother say?"

"You know my mother, she won't ever go against Father. She didn't want me to go to college in the first place. She wants me to get married."

"I know they aren't the most loving people in the world, I just can't believe they don't see how talented you are. They should be encouraging your painting."

"Derrick, I've missed talking to you." Laura grinned and hugged him tightly. "I wish I could introduce you to Danette. She would really like you."

"It sounds like the two of you have become very close friends."

"I love her, Derrick. She is so smart, and loyal, and she's beautiful."

"I am glad you found someone to talk to."

"So am I. She is pretty special."

"We had better go back to the party before someone comes looking for us."

"Thanks, Derrick."

"You're welcome doll, now smile so that everyone thinks you are having a good time." He tickled her as they entered the crowed room.

It was well after one in the morning when the telephone rang by Danette's head. She hadn't been sound asleep but the ringing of the telephone by her head disturbed her restlessness.

"Hello."

"Danette, its Laura." Laura's voice was barely above a whisper.

"Laura, is everything all right? Are you okay?"

"No, I'm not, Danette. I miss you so much, I just want to come home."

"I miss you, too. I can't believe how much. Laura, are you and Derrick getting back together?" Danette's voice betrayed her feelings.

"Never, Danette! My parents are pressuring me but I'm not in love with Derrick and he certainly is not in love with me. I'm coming back as soon as possible."

"I'm glad, Laura."

"Danette, I love you," Laura whispered nervously.

"I love you, Laura. Good night, and I am so glad you called," Danette whispered back.

"I'll call you Christmas Eve, okay?"

"I'll be waiting."

"Bye, Dani."

Danette's heart beat wildly as she hung up the telephone. She felt wonderful and terrible all at the same time. These feelings were different then anything she had ever felt. Unknown to Danette, Laura was examining her feelings in the very same way. They were both overwhelmed and totally lost.

The next few days flew by for Danette as she went to work early and stayed late just to keep herself busy. Her aunt had asked her to do some computer support work at the company over the Christmas break. Danette didn't mind. The work was easy and it kept her busy while she earned some spending money. It also kept her from thinking about Laura twenty-four hours a day. Her feelings were still all mixed up but she just pushed them away. It would soon be Christmas Eve and Laura had promised to call.

Laura was not having as easy a time as Danette. Her father was pressuring her to quit school and come home.

"Laura, it would be different if you were attending an Ivy League school and majoring in something worthwhile. But this art hobby of yours is not going to amount to anything." Victor Benson, Laura's father was seated behind his massive desk having summoned Laura to his office. "I don't know why you couldn't study something that counted."

"Father, you promised as long as I got a scholarship I could go to the college of my choice. I have only been there one quarter. You must let me stay. I am learning so much." She pleaded with him.

"It is such a waste of time. Your mother and I did not spend all that money on a private school for you to throw it all away. What good will an art degree do you? You have a duty to this family. You will marry into an acceptable family and be the perfect wife and mother. It is what your mother and I expect of you."

"Father, I know you want me to marry, but can't it wait until after college?"

"Why do you want to waste four years? Derrick is ready to get married."

"Father, how many times do I have to explain this to you. Derrick and I are not going to marry each other."

"I don't understand what you find objectionable about Derrick."

"There is nothing wrong with Derrick, I don't want to marry him and he doesn't want to marry me."

"If you just put out an effort. It would be the perfect match. It is what your mother and I want. You wouldn't have to work. Derrick will be extremely wealthy"

"I don't care about Derrick's money."

"You certainly should. It will keep you in clothes and jewelry."

"I don't care about clothes and jewelry. You want me to be just like Mother. Never expressing an opinion other than yours, attending all those charity events so that you and your business can look generous and caring, always wearing the perfect clothes, and showing up at the required parties." Laura's voice shook with anger.

"Young lady, that is enough! I will not stand for your attitude." Laura's father had risen from his chair, obviously as angry as his daughter. His voice had become very loud.

"Father, I'm not trying to argue with you. I am just reminding you of your promise. I am going back to school."

"Fine young lady, you go play for four years. However, be prepared to marry and take your place in this family when you are through playing. Your mother and I will be expecting nothing less. It is what your mother did and you will do the same." It was spoken as a command.

"Yes, Father." Laura knew better then to argue any more. She was through trying to talk to her father. She had been trying for years and knew that pushing him when he was angry just made everything worse. Her heart hurt as she shook her head in agreement. She knew she could never do what he asked.

"Laura, your mother and I would be very pleased if you and Derrick would announce your engagement this Christmas Eve. You just need to convince him that you want to marry him."

"Father, how many times do I have to tell you. Derrick and I are just friends. We are never going to marry each other. We are not in love with each other."

"What's love got to do with it? The marriage would be a good match. You both come from solid old families. I know Derrick's parents want this to happen as much as your mother and I do."

"But I told you, Father, I don't love Derrick and I'm not going to marry someone I don't love."

"Laura, you must give up this idealistic attitude of yours. Do you think your mother and I were madly in love with each other when we married? We respected each other and recognized that the match would be advantageous to both families. Your mother's duty was to marry well. We have had a mutually satisfying relationship for many years."

"Mutually satisfying relationship? That is why mother spends your money as fast as you make it. She never talks about anything important or meaningful, just parties and clothes, and you spend all your time working, buying and destroying company after company. You love your business and your money more than your family and I can't live like that. I need love and passion in my life!" Laura pleaded trying to make him understand.

"Passion, that's bunk. I don't know where you learned all this nonsense. You need a strong husband who knows how to control your life for you." His voice had risen in volume again.

Laura's mother burst into the study, indignation on her voice. "Victor, do you need to speak so loudly, I can hear you all the way in the sitting room. The help can hear every word. Can you not lower your voice?"

"Yes dear, Laura and I are finished with our discussion." Laura's father dismissed her with a wave of his hand.

"Good, dear. Laura needs to take a nap before the party this evening so she will look rested and pretty for Derrick." Laura's mother ushered her to the door.

"Remember, Father, you promised as long as I have my scholarship I can stay at the University. I am going to hold you to that promise."

"Come along Laura, don't bother your father anymore with this nonsense. You take yourself upstairs and rest now. I will have Jennifer wake you up in time to bathe and dress." Laura's mother continued to direct Laura down the hall toward the main stairwell.

"Fine, Mother, I will rest." Laura sighed with impatience. Experience had taught her not to try to discuss anything of a serious nature with her mother. She would just evade and send her to her father. When she became agitated, she would claim a headache and hide in her bedroom for days on end.

"Thank you, now I believe I will do the same."

Laura slowly climbed the stairwell toward her bedroom. Even after eighteen years she still was unable to understand her mother and father. They in turn, had no clue as to who their daughter had become.

Her mother had come from a very wealthy family and never attended any school beyond private high school. She had married Victor at nineteen, having just been presented as a debutante. Her father was seventeen years older than her mother, but he had come from a very wealthy family. Laura's mother immediately accepted his proposal. It had been an arranged marriage, one that suited both families involved.

Since Laura could remember, her mother spent most of her time working on charity events or hosting her father's business functions. Beyond that, her only other interests were her continuous remodeling of their one hundred-year-old home and shopping in the most expensive clothing stores. Laura had also recognized at an early age that she would not receive any meaningful affection from either of her parents. Thankfully, she had received much love and attention from Richard, her father's chauffeur, and Rachel his wife, the housekeeper. It was their attention and love that she had turned to when the trials of growing up in such a barren home had been too much for her. As she had gained in age and maturity, she found security in doing well at school and in her art classes. Painting became her passion, something she could do in the privacy of her own room.

That is where she went now. She could shut out her parents' world even for a short time. She was so very lonely and missed Danette very much. Danette and her aunt had become her true family. They showed their love for each other with much affection and this love had included Laura. She could be herself around them and that was worth everything to her. As she hid out in her room she wondered what Danette was doing at that moment.

"Merry Christmas, Danette!"

"Thanks Peter thanks Michael, Merry Christmas to you both. Have you seen my aunt yet?" Aunt Dorothy's annual Christmas Eve party had begun and her condominium was packed with friends and employees she had known for years. Every year the party got larger and more crowded.

"No, we haven't seen her yet, but wait until you see what Peter made her for Christmas."

"Let's go find her, she'll be so excited, she loves presents." Pushing their way through the crowd of well wishers, they could see Danette's aunt standing in the center of the living room surrounded by people.

"Aunt Dorothy, look who's here!"

"Peter, Michael, Merry Christmas! You both look very festive. Do you want something to eat or drink? You must try everything, Marie outdid herself." Like a breath of fresh air, Danette's Aunt Dorothy hugged both men, kissed them on their cheeks, and patted them both on their backs. Danette's aunt loved every one and she wasn't afraid to show it. In return, everyone who came in contact with her returned her love.

"Are you boys having a good Christmas?"

"Yes, Dorothy, and how about yours?" Michael replied.

"I'm having a wonderful Christmas with all my family and friends here. What more could I wish for?" Slipping her arm around Danette, Dorothy hugged her tightly.

"Speaking of Christmas, we have a present for you, or should I say Peter has a present for you." Michael stated with a grin.

"What is it?" Dorothy asked, excitement in her voice.

"It's out in the entry way. It was too heavy to carry around," Peter responded. "Do you want to see it now?"

"Yes, let's go!" With Aunt Dorothy leading the parade like a tugboat, the four of them wound their way back to the front door. Aunt Dorothy stopped to say something to nearly every person she saw. It was a long trip. Upon reaching the entry, Peter stepped over to a draped figure in the corner. It stood about three feet tall and, with a little flourish, Peter pulled the drape off to expose a most exquisite statue. It was a carving in the form of a woman with a flowing dress and long wavy hair. The gown on the woman appeared almost opaque; it had been sculpted with such skill. Both Danette and her Aunt Dorothy were speechless. They were stunned with its beauty.

"It's gorgeous, Peter!" Aunt Dorothy exclaimed. "I have never seen anything like it before. Such talent!"

"Peter, it's fantastic, when did you do it? It must have taken you months." Danette raved. She was as overwhelmed as her aunt was.

"I have been working on it for awhile. It did turn out nicely, didn't it?" Peter replied with a grin.

"Thank you, what a wonderful gift." Aunt Dorothy hugged them again. "I think I will put it in the entry to my office so that I can see it every day. Come, let's move it into the living room where everyone can see it now." Peter picked up the sculpture and followed Dorothy, the crowd swallowing them both up.

"Michael, I can't believe how talented Peter is!" Danette exclaimed.

"He is good, isn't he?" Michael boasted with a grin. "Have you heard from Laura?" he asked.

"She called two nights ago while Aunt Dorothy and I were at The Nutcracker. I missed her call. I miss her."

"Maybe she'll call tonight, since it is Christmas Eve," Michael replied, giving Danette a quick hug.

"I hope so."

They spent the rest of the evening singing Christmas Carols and visiting with all of their friends. Well after midnight when Peter, Michael, Danette, and Dorothy were just cleaning up the last of the mess, the telephone rang.

"Now who could that be calling this late?" Aunt Dorothy remarked as Danette picked up the receiver.

"Hello." Danette answered.

"Merry Christmas, Danette." It was Laura.

"What are you doing calling so late? It's after three in the morning back there." Danette responded, her heart pounding in her chest. "Merry Christmas to you. Peter and Michael are here, and Aunt Dorothy. They all wish you a Merry Christmas. Here, Michael wants to say hello."

"Hi girl, when are you coming home? Peter and I miss you something terrible."

"Soon Michael. I miss you all so much, I wish I was there right now."

"Are you having a Merry Christmas with your parents?"

"It's okay. I'll tell you all about it when I get back. Give Peter a big hug and kiss for me."

"You know I will. We love you, Laura."

"I love you guys, too."

"Here's Danette again, see you soon!"

"Hi." Danette spoke softly into the telephone.

"Hi, how are you doing?" Laura inquired, equally as quietly.

"I'm fine, how is your visit going?"

"Okay. It's nice to see some of my old friends, but I'd rather be there. My father is trying to talk me into transferring to a school back here."

Danette remained silent. What if Laura never came back, what would she do? "Laura, are you thinking of transferring?" Danette asked quickly, her heart pounding in her throat. Michael, Peter, and her aunt had left the room. She could hear them laughing in the kitchen.

"No, I'm not thinking of transferring. I miss you all so much. I love you guys. Danette, I love you."

"I love you too." Danette replied. "We all miss you very much." Especially me, she thought. "Hurry back and, Laura, Merry Christmas."

"Merry Christmas to you, I wish I was there."

"I wish you were, too. Call again, if you get a chance."

"I will, take care, Danette."

"You too. Good bye."

"Bye."

One more week, Danette couldn't believe how much she missed Laura. She just would have to keep herself very busy. She would go to work with her aunt everyday. That would keep her busy. She would work right up until New Year's Eve.

Chapter 6

"Danette, get out of here," cried Dorothy's secretary Beth. "You've been here all week, working from dawn until dusk. Go home! You are too young to work this hard. Besides, it's New Year's Eve."

"I'll go in a little bit, I'm going to pick up Laura at the airport. She's flying in at six-thirty tonight." Danette replied, her nose all but stuck to the computer screen. "Your computer should be okay now, Beth. I cleaned up some of the files. Let me know if you have any problems with it."

"You know I won't." Beth responded with a chuckle, " Where do you learn all this stuff? In college?"

"A little bit. I enjoy working with computers and I really liked all my classes I took. I just wish I could take more real business courses. I have to take all these pre-major classes. What a waste." Impatience could be heard in Danette's voice.

"Danette, there's a good reason for taking all those classes. Not all kids are as single-minded as you are. Many people your age don't know what they want to major in and taking preliminary courses helps them decide. You are the most ambitious person I know besides your aunt. I remember when she used to bring you to work with her when you were very young. Even then you said you were going to be just like your Aunt Dorothy."

Danette grinned at Beth. She had known Beth all her life. When her parents died and her aunt had taken her in, Beth had taken it upon herself to make sure both Dorothy and Danette were being taken care of. She remembered every birthday, anniversary, and special occasion. When Danette had graduated from high school Beth had sat next to Aunt Dorothy and was just as proud and happy. Danette had come to rely on Beth's opinions as much as Dorothy did.

"Okay, okay, I think I will take your advice and get out of here. I'll go home and take a nice hot bath. Have a happy New Year!"

"You too, sweetheart, and be careful tonight. No drinking and driving."

"I will be careful, Beth, thanks." Hugging Beth quickly, Danette grabbed her jacket and started for the door. "Can you say good-bye to Aunt Dorothy for me?"

"Sure doll, now get out of here." Beth replied, shooing her away.

"Bye!" Out the door Danette popped. She did spend a moment admiring Peter's sculpture. Her Aunt Dorothy, as promised, had installed it in the front lobby of her office for all to appreciate. Peter had already received several telephone calls from some of her Aunt's friends asking if he had more pieces for sale. Peter was ecstatic and Danette was very happy for him.

The clock read six-fifteen and the plane was still due at six-thirty. Danette had checked three times. She was so nervous her stomach was tied in knots. She couldn't explain the feeling, but she was so excited to see Laura again she could barely stand still. She had missed her terribly. Laura had become a part of her family. Now all she had to do was wait fifteen more minutes and it was killing her.

"Flight five eighty-three from New York City is now disembarking at gate N thirty-three." The flight had finally arrived. In moments, Laura would be stepping off the plane. As the first few people filtered out, Danette held her breath. What if Laura didn't miss her as much as Danette had? Was there something wrong with Danette? Was what she was feeling normal?

"Danette."

She heard her name being called. Looking at the crowd of people now exiting the gate she couldn't see Laura. Where was she? She scanned the crowd unable to locate her. Just as Danette scanned the gate again, the crowd cleared and Laura was standing in the center of the aisle with a huge smile on face. She was looking right at Danette. Still holding her breath, Danette started to walk toward her as Laura began to walk in her direction. When they reached each other, Danette paused, unsure, as how to greet her, but Laura didn't hesitate. She threw her arms around Danette and hugged her tightly.

"Oh, I missed you so much," Laura whispered as she tightened her hold.

Finally taking her first breath, Danette responded, wrapping her arms around Laura. She whispered back, "Not as much as I missed you. I'm so glad you're back." They stood there several minutes hugging each other tightly, oblivious of everyone around them. Danette could smell the light floral scent that she knew was Laura. She could feel Laura's breath upon her neck. Danette felt so complete standing there hugging her.

"Excuse me." Someone was trying to get by them.

"We had better get out of the way," Laura whispered. Giving Danette one last squeeze, Laura started to pull away. At the last second she gave Danette a short kiss on her cheek. Danette's heart pounded and her stomach fluttered.

"Sure, did you check your luggage?" Danette responded quickly, still feeling anxious.

"Yes, let's go get it and get out of here." Laura answered, putting her arm through Danette's.

Forty minutes later, Danette and Laura sat in Aunt Dorothy's car on their way out of the airport parking lot. "Peter and Michael are going to pick us up at eight to go on the cruise tonight. I told them to pick us up from the dormitory. I thought we could go back there. I don't have to return my Aunt's car until tomorrow afternoon.

"Great, we can exchange Christmas presents before we go out."

"Okay, but are you hungry?" Danette asked.

"Not really, I had dinner on the plane. How about you? You never eat," Laura chided her with a grin.

"I want you to know I did have a sandwich before I left for the airport, so I have eaten," Danette replied laughing. Laura knew all her bad habits. "How was Christmas with your family? Were they glad to see you?"

"I suppose so. My father did his best to talk me into transferring to a school back there. I had to remind him of his promise. Now all I have to do is keep my grades up and I can stay in school here."

"You know you're going to get straight A's." Danette responded. "I've never seen anyone work as hard as you do."

"No, only you! By the way, when do we get our grades?"

"They should arrive some time next week by mail. Let's not worry about it now. Wait until you see the sculpture Peter gave Aunt Dorothy for Christmas. It is so beautiful. She put it in the lobby of her office. In fact, several people have called Peter to see if he has any other pieces for sale. It's a statue of a woman."

"I know, I watched him working on it at the studio. It is something, isn't it! He really is talented," Laura said with a smile. "Wait till you see what he made for you!"

"What, tell me," Danette begged. Laura knew Danette liked surprises.

"You'll just have to wait." Laura grinned. They laughed and giggled all the way to the dorm.

"What do you have in here, books?" Danette asked, as she dragged Laura's suitcase into the elevator.

"Just a few things, a couple of Christmas presents, some new clothes," Laura responded chuckling.

"I bet just a few things." Danette laughed as she struggled down the hall to their room. Laura watched her laughing. Unlocking the door, Danette lifted the suitcase onto Laura's bed and then collapsed onto her own. "I'm exhausted."

"You're such a wimp, Danette." Laura laughed as she flopped onto her bed next to the suitcase. "I guess you don't want your Christmas present."

"What is it?" Danette asked, sitting up quickly. "Let me get yours." Reaching under her desk she pulled out a package wrapped in red foil paper and tied with a white ribbon. "Here, open this first."

"How about I put my clothes away and then we open our presents," Laura responded.

"Okay, I'll change my clothes for the party while you're unpacking,"

Ten minutes later both Laura and Danette sat side by side on Danette's bed. Laura's bed was still covered with clothes. She had never quite managed the art of organization that Danette had.

"Open yours first," Danette requested.

"How about we open them together," Laura suggested.

"No, you open yours first, please." Danette pleaded with her.

"Okay, here goes." Ripping the paper and ribbon off the package, Laura rapidly opened the box. Inside were two more wrapped packages. Choosing the flat one first, Laura proceeded to unwrap a book. It was a book of Georgia O'Keefe's photographs. She was Laura's favorite artist. "This is wonderful, Danette, I love it, thank you!" she exclaimed. "She's my favorite!" Laura announced, leafing through the book.

"I know, now open your other present. You can look at the book later."

"Okay, okay," Laura said with laugh," What can this be?" she asked as she picked up the second package. Tearing the wrapping off, Laura found an ornately carved wooden box with a metal clasp.

"What a beautiful box."

"Open it, the present is inside." Danette whispered, excitement in her voice. Slipping the latch, Laura lifted the lid. Lying in satin lined sections were twelve watercolor brushes with carved handles.

"It's a Japanese brush set. Each brush is handmade from sable hair and each handle is carved with good luck symbols. According to the woman I purchased it from, they are only given to the best artists. It is said that true art flows from these brushes."

Laura, upon opening the case had bowed her head and not uttered a word. "Don't you like it, Laura?" Danette asked, her voice trembling.

"Oh, Danette, I love it, it's perfect." Laura lifted her head and looked at Danette. Danette noticed the tears rolling down Laura's cheeks.

"Then why are you crying?" Danette asked feeling even worse. Putting her hand on Laura's shoulder, she tried to get her to answer. Laura just kept on crying, tears dripping off her chin.

"Laura, I'm sorry, whatever I did, I'm sorry. Please don't cry." Danette was ready to cry herself. She had no idea what she had done.

"Danette, I'm crying because I'm happy," Laura whispered, with tears in her eyes and a smile on her face. Throwing her arms around Danette's neck and hugging her tightly she whispered, "I can't believe you got this for me. My parents think my painting is a waste of time, a nice hobby. You are the only one I know who understands how important it is to me. I can't thank you enough."

With that confession Laura squeezed her arms around Danette even tighter. Danette returned the hug, knowing she had found the perfect gift for Laura. Her heart felt wonderful. She liked making Laura happy.

"Thank you," Laura whispered. She turned her face into Danette's and lightly kissed her on the lips. Before Danette could react, Laura pulled away.

"Now it's your turn, open your present." Laura said, with a smile. Danette was still sitting quietly. The kiss Laura had placed on her lips had affected her more than she was willing to admit. Something was wrong with her she was attracted to Laura!

"Danette, open your present," Laura teased.

Interrupting her disturbing thoughts, Danette picked up the small package Laura had placed on her lap. She would deal with her mixed up feelings later. She would enjoy opening her present now. Slowly she unfolded the gold and green wrapping paper from a small package, to reveal a jeweler's box. Gently she lifted the lid and lying in the center was a gold necklace with a gold medallion attached to it. On the face of the medallion was etched a woman very similar to the sculpture Peter had given to her aunt. The woman had long flowing robes, curly long hair, and a classic profile. It was very dainty and absolutely beautiful. She had never seen anything like it.

"It's Helen of Troy. She was supposed to have been a brilliant, strong woman. She reminded me of you," Laura said quietly. "Turn it over."

Slowly Danette turned the medallion over, overwhelmed by the words Laura had spoken. She had a lump in her throat. On the back of the medallion there was engraved in delicate flowing script the following: " To someone very special, love Laura." Danette was still unable to respond. She now felt like crying.

"I love it!" She whispered to Laura. "I'll wear it always. Thank you."

"You're welcome," Laura responded with a smile. "I'm glad you like it. I also have another present for you. Close your eyes. I'll tell you when to open them."

Danette did what she was asked, closing her eyes, still holding the box in her lap. She didn't need another present. The necklace was perfect!

"Are your eyes closed?" Laura called from across the room.

"Yes," Danette replied, giggling.

"Don't peek."

"I'm not." There were some rustling sounds and then Danette heard Laura speak. "Okay, you can open your eyes now."

Danette opened her eyes to find Laura standing in front of her holding a large painting. Danette could see it was one of Laura's. It had beautiful flowers and jungle-like plants painted with vibrant colors. It was one of her best.

"This is for me?" Danette asked, standing up to come closer to the painting. The plants all looked alive, like they were growing off the canvas. Laura was very talented. "I can't believe it, you are giving me this painting. Are you sure?"

"I painted it for you. Don't you like it?" Laura questioned with a worried look on her face.

"I love it. I can't believe you painted it for me! You're so talented, this is fantastic!"

A knock on their door interrupted them. "Danette, Laura, are you in there?" It was Michael.

"What time is it?" Laura remarked. "They must be here to pick us up for the party." She walked over to open the door. "Michael, come in we're almost ready."

"Hey Laura, give me a hug! Welcome home, we missed you."

"I missed you guys. Where's Peter?" She asked hugging him in return.

"He's out in the car freezing. Dress warmly, it's cold out there," Michael responded. "Come on Danette, aren't you gals ready to go?"

"Just one minute and I'll be ready." Danette leaned the painting against the closet. She didn't want to share it with Michael yet. She did want to wear the medallion and, when Michael turned his attention back to Laura asking her all sorts of questions about her trip back East, Danette pulled the medallion from its box and unfastened the clasp. Reaching behind her neck she refastened it. "Okay, let's go, folks."

The three of them left the dorm room on their way to the New Year's Eve cruise. More hugs were exchanged between Laura and Peter as the four of them were finally on their way. It would be a night Laura and Danette would never forget. The boat was full of people and, as it pulled out of the dock on Lake Washington, the four braved the cold and watched the lights of the city drift by. They were all looking forward to New Year's Eve and more importantly the New Year.

"Let's go get something to eat," Peter requested. "I'm hungry!"

"You are always hungry," Michael responded with a laugh. "Let's go find some food for this starving guy."

"I think I'll stay here for a moment," Laura remarked. " I want to enjoy the view for a few more moments. Danette, would you stay with me please?"

"Sure I'd love to, we'll catch up with you guys later, okay?" Danette asked.

"Okay, we'll see you inside."

As Peter and Michael left, Danette turned to Laura and found her looking directly at her. Something was happening between the two of them. Danette wasn't sure what it was, but something was different, and Danette was scared. Even now, her heart was pounding. Laura had a smile on her face and she looked beautiful standing next to Danette. Her long dark hair was swirling loose around her shoulders, her large brown eyes glowing in the dark. Danette had never seen anyone so beautiful. She liked everything about her, the way she laughed, the way she painted, the way she walked, and talked. All of a sudden, it dawned on Danette what was wrong. She was in love with Laura! She couldn't let Laura know how she felt, it was wrong! It was okay for Peter and Michael but not for Danette. She wasn't gay. Her feelings were all wrong. If Laura found out how Danette was feeling she would hate her!

"Danette, why such a sad look? It's New Year's and we're spending it together, what could possibly be better," Laura said, touching Danette's cheek with her fingers. "Is something wrong?" She inquired softly.

Reaching up, Danette captured Laura's fingers with hers. "Nothing's wrong, you're right, what could be more perfect?"

Laura was still looking directly into Danette's eyes, her fingers being held tightly by Danette. In fact, Danette thought she could feel Laura squeezing her fingers in return. Danette could hear her own heart pounding. It was so loud Laura could probably hear it also. As Danette kept looking at her, Laura's fingers definitely tightened around Danette's. Laura moved closer to Danette, leaning in to her almost as if she was going to kiss her. Danette moved closer to Laura, not thinking about what was happening, her body reacting to the physical pull of Laura.

"Hey girls, you should hear the music inside, it's great for dancing." Michael's voice could be heard from behind them. Danette pulled back, jerking her hand out of Laura's, her face flooding with embarrassment.

"Where's Peter?" Laura asked, turning herself around to greet Michael.

"He's eating at the food table, where else would he be! I swear I don't know how he stays so slim. He eats all the time." Michael rattled on oblivious to the fact that both Laura and Danette were not responding to his remarks. Danette looked quickly at Laura, wondering if she had imagined everything. Laura was looking directly at Michael. She didn't appear to be the slightest bit different or uncomfortable.

"Aren't you gals cold? You've been outside for quite awhile."

Danette didn't feel cold, in fact, she felt very warm. "I guess we should go inside. What do you think, Laura?"

Danette couldn't bring herself to look at her again. She wasn't really sure what had just happened between the two of them. Maybe nothing happened. Maybe Danette was mistaken. She was terribly confused.

"Sure, I'm hungry myself, let's go find Peter, before he eats all the good stuff," Laura said with a laugh. Linking one arm with Michael's and her other with Danette's, she pulled them along with her. Danette was even more convinced that nothing had happened between her and Laura. Pasting a smile on her face, Danette decided to forget everything and enjoy the rest of the evening.

"Fifteen minutes until midnight and counting," The disk jockey announced. The four of them had been dancing for over two hours, laughing and giggling the entire time. They all were having great fun.

"Do you have a hat?" Peter asked Danette, grinning at her with a silver tiara attached to his head. She couldn't help but giggle.

"I've got one," she laughed, "Where did Laura and Michael go?"

"They went to get us champagne for the toast. Are you having a good time, Danette?" Peter inquired.

"I'm having a great time, aren't you?" She responded, smiling at him. "Who wouldn't be, spending New Year's with her best friends." She hugged him. " I love you guys."

"Are you sure everything's okay? You've been awfully quiet tonight?" Peter asked, concern on his face.

"I'm fine," she replied, feeling guilty. She knew she hadn't been herself. "I'm just a little tired, that's all."

"Are you sure? You know if you ever need someone to talk to, I'm always here." Peter volunteered giving her a hug.

"Thanks, Peter, I know that. I'm fine really." She hugged him in return, ignoring the feeling of guilt. She didn't know where to start. She wasn't sure what was wrong her and that certainly was not a good way to start the New Year.

"Here you go, Peter." Michael spoke up behind them. "Champagne to celebrate. Danette, Laura has yours." Just as he spoke, Laura walked up.

"Put your hats on guys, it's almost midnight!" You could hear the excitement in Laura's voice as she handed Danette her glass of champagne. "I can't remember having a better New Year's Eve, being with the three people I love the most. It's perfect!" Her voice had lowered to almost a whisper, her eyes sparkling as she smiled. Danette didn't even look at Peter and Michael. Laura and her excitement mesmerized Danette.

"Three, two, one, Happy New Year!" The announcer yelled over the speakers.

Out of the corner of her eye Danette could see Michael and Peter embracing. Turning directly toward Laura, she was surprised to see Laura looking back at her, her brown eyes glistening in the dark.

Without saying a word, Laura stepped toward Danette and Danette leaned into her, both of them wrapping their arms around each other. Danette's heart pounded in her chest and her stomach fluttered with anticipation. Laura tightened her arms around Danette's neck and, as everyone around them celebrated the New Year with hugs and kisses, they held on to each other tightly. Danette buried her face into the side of Laura's neck. She wanted to memorize the scent that she knew was Laura. She didn't want the moment to end. Danette could feel Laura's face against her cheek and she wanted so desperately to understand her feelings.

Whispering to Laura as she tightened her arms even more snugly around her, "Happy New Year Laura, I love you."

"I love you, Danette, so very much."

As Laura whispered, she moved her face closer to Danette's. Danette could feel Laura's lips against her cheek and Danette couldn't stop herself as she moved her lips to meet Laura's. As if it were planned, their lips met in a kiss, not a simple friendly kiss, but a deep passionate one. Not thinking of or noticing everyone around them, they deepened the kiss, tasting each other's lips for the very first time. A balloon burst close to them, and with a gasp they pulled away from each other. Danette released her breath in a loud sigh. Looking back at Laura, she didn't know what to say to her. The look on Laura's face was so serious.

"Laura, are you okay?" Danette asked softly, afraid of the answer.

"Yes, Danette, are you?" Laura whispered back, her eyes large and questioning.

"Oh Laura, I'm fine." She reached her hand out to Laura involuntarily. Laura clasped Danette's hand with her own, their fingers interlocking.

"Danette, we need to talk," Laura stated softly, her eyes watching Danette carefully.

"I know," Danette responded. "Everything will be okay, don't worry." Danette wanted to make sure she hadn't frightened her. She couldn't lose Laura's friendship.

"Hey girls, its New Year's, why so serious?" Michael questioned, interrupting their conversation.

"Happy New Year," Laura responded with a smile. "Come here and give me a hug." Danette and Peter exchanged hugs and kisses, and with much laughter they exchanged partners and hugged again.

"Come on girls, let's dance the rest of the night away!" Peter yelled. Michael, Laura, and Danette couldn't resist his enthusiasm. They all laughed and followed him to the dance floor.

Two hours later Peter pulled his Volkswagen into the driveway of the dormitory. The four of them had laughed and giggled on the drive home. As they had gotten closer to the dormitory, Danette had become increasingly nervous. She knew she and Laura needed to talk, but she was so scared. Maybe she had frightened Laura. What if Laura didn't want to have anything more to do with her? Danette couldn't even imagine the possibility. It would break her heart.

"Thanks for driving, Peter," Danette stated, hugging him from the back seat. "I had a wonderful time."

"You're welcome sweetie, any time! It was fun, wasn't it?" Peter replied.

"What better way to celebrate than with our two favorite people." Michael chimed in.

"Thanks for inviting us, it was terrific." Laura agreed as Michael got out to let her and Danette out of the car.

"Hurry up and get inside, before you get cold," Michael advised as he quickly hugged them both. "Don't forget football and dinner tomorrow and we're going to exchange Christmas gifts."

"Okay," Laura and Danette both responded as they walked swiftly to the front door. Laura unlocked the door and they both entered. Danette turned to wave to Michael and Peter as they drove off. Slowly she turned back to look at Laura.

"Boy, it is cold." It was all Danette could think of saying. She was shaking she was so nervous.

"Let's hurry upstairs," Laura suggested quietly. They both stepped into the elevator side by side. Danette couldn't even look at Laura she was so scared. Laura was never this quiet. She always visited with Danette. Something was seriously wrong. The elevator door opened up on their floor and they both walked to their room without a word. Opening the door, Laura stepped in and Danette followed her. Danette shut the door and turned toward Laura. She had walked over to their window and was looking out with her back toward Danette.

"Laura, would you like to talk now?" Danette asked softly, afraid of the answer. She was terrified.

"Yes, I would like to, if you're not too tired?" Laura replied quietly, her back still to Danette. "I need to tell you something."

Danette's heart was in her throat. "Okay." She still didn't move, she was frozen in place. She could see Laura's profile against the window but she couldn't tell what expression was on her face. She waited for Laura to speak.

"I don't know how to start." Laura voice was very soft. "When I met you, I knew you were special and I knew we would be best friends. It was like I had known you forever."

Danette shook her head in agreement. "I know I felt the same way." Danette responded to Laura, speaking equally as quietly.

"Please just listen to me. If I don't finish this now, I might not ever have the courage again." Laura pleaded as she turned around to Danette.

Danette could see that she was crying. She wanted to go to her and comfort her but she remained where she was waiting for Laura to speak. Her heart ached as she looked at her.

"I have been feeling different lately and I need to tell you." Laura started again. Danette held her breath, expecting the worst.

"When I went home for Christmas I realized something." Laura paused and took a deep breath. "I realized that I missed you more than you could know." Danette continued to hold her breath.

"Danette, I've fallen in love with you." Laura blurted out as she hung her head down, her hands clasped tightly in front of her.

"Laura." Danette moved quickly to stand in front of her. Reaching out, she lifted Laura's chin up so they were looking at each other. Laura had tears streaming down her cheeks. "Please don't cry." Danette pleaded. "I feel the same way." Danette had also begun to cry.

"You do?" Laura asked, her eyes wide with disbelief.

"Yes," Danette responded. With her fingers she started to wipe the tears from Laura's face. Laura reached up and grabbed Danette's hand. She pulled it to her lips and brushed the fingers with a kiss. As she kissed Danette's fingers, she stepped toward Danette, slipping her other arm around Danette's waist. Danette responded by moving closer to Laura, wanting to hold her. As if Laura could read her mind, she pulled Danette tightly to her and Danette knew she was going to kiss her. Danette wanted her to. She could feel her body tingle everywhere Laura's body touched hers. Danette knew this was right, it felt so perfect. She turned her face toward Laura and, bending toward her, they kissed. Danette wrapped her arms around Laura and tightened her embrace. She never wanted it to end. Laura's kiss took her breath away. Laura's lips had parted and Danette could feel her tongue against her lips. Opening her lips to Laura's tongue, she sucked lightly on it. Laura responded with a quiet moan as Danette began to taste Laura's lips by tracing them with her tongue.

They couldn't get enough of each other. Laura began to spread light kisses across Danette's cheek and down her neck. She nuzzled Danette's ear, flicking her tongue lightly along the edge. A gasp escaped Danette's lips as Laura continued her exploration of Danette. Danette decided to return the favor as she spread soft quick kisses along Laura's chin and down her neck. She continued to kiss Laura along the edge of her blouse to the first button. She paused to look at Laura. Laura's eyes had become a soft chocolate brown and heavy lidded. She was beautiful.

As Danette bent toward Laura again, she could feel Laura's hands against the bare skin of her back. Her skin was on fire where Laura's hands came in contact with her. It was a glorious feeling. She could feel Laura's heart beating as she reached up and slowly unbuttoned her top button.

"Danette," Laura whispered, "You are so beautiful. I've been wanting to kiss you for so long."

"I've been wanting you to kiss me," Danette responded, kissing Laura deeply. Danette again left a trail of kisses along Laura's chin and, with little flicks of her tongue she could taste the texture and flavor of Laura's skin. As she reached the top of Laura's breast with her lips, Danette hesitated, unsure of what to do. Laura's arms tightened around Danette. Sliding her hands down Danette's back, she slipped her hands around Danette's waist. Gliding her hands up she slowly cupped them around Danette's breasts. Danette held her breath. She wanted Laura to continue touching her. She wanted to touch Laura also. She began to unbutton the rest of Laura's blouse. She followed the line of Laura's bra with her lips. Sliding the shirt open, she slid it off Laura's shoulders. Laura slid Danette's shirt up and over her head, throwing it on the floor. They embraced tightly, savoring the feel of their skin against each other. Laura ran her hands up and down Danette's back, touching every part of her skin. Slowly she unclasped Danette's bra. Reaching up she slid the straps down Danette's shoulders. As it slipped down between them to the floor, Laura smothered Danette's shoulder blade with soft kisses. Laura's lips continued to blaze a trail down Danette's breast until they captured Danette's nipple. Danette's body flooded with warmth as Laura began to lightly suck and taste her. Danette could not prevent the moan that escaped from her as her body melted against Laura. As Laura paid equal attention to her other breast with her lips and tongue, Danette felt weak in her knees. Laura continued her passionate journey and Danette had lost all reason. She needed to kiss Laura like she had been kissed. She wanted to make Laura feel like she did. Reaching down, she lifted Laura's head up and kissed her with all the love and passion she felt inside her. As Danette continued to kiss Laura she slid both hands up and across Laura's ribs to the edge of her bra. Hesitating slightly, she was unsure whether to continue.

"Danette, please don't stop," Laura's husky voice requested," I want you to touch me, I need you to." Danette's stomach fluttered as she responded to Laura's plea.

"I don't want to stop, I want to touch you everywhere. I love how you feel and taste. I love you," Danette murmured as she slid her hands around Laura to unclasp her bra. Laura helped her by taking it off and letting it slide to the floor. As Laura stood there Danette couldn't help but stare. She has seen Laura undressed before but never like this. Laura began to blush as Danette continued to admire her.

"You are beautiful, Laura."

"Oh Danette, I am not," Laura responded, wrapping her arms around Danette.

"Yes, you are." Danette replied as she embraced Laura.

She kissed her neck, nuzzling her ear, and again slid her hands up until she had captured both of Laura's breasts. Her skin was as soft as satin. With the tips of her fingers, Danette brushed both nipples and felt them tighten. She traced both of them with her fingertips until she could wait no longer. Bending her head down, she touched Laura's nipple with the tip of her tongue. A small cry escaped from Laura as she tightened her arms around Danette, pulling her even closer. Danette continued to spread kisses on both Laura's breasts. She wrapped her arms around Laura, slid her hands down Laura's back, and pulled her even closer. She wanted to get as close as possible.

"Danette, come with me." Laura whispered. She took Danette's hand and led her to Danette's bed. She slowly pushed Danette back until she was seated on the bed. Standing in front of Danette, Laura stepped as close as she could get to Danette without touching her. Danette reached out with both arms toward Laura.

"Danette, I need to say something to you and I can't talk with you touching me. I can't even think when you touch me," Laura whispered with a slight smile on her face.

"I know, I can't think when you touch me either," Danette admitted.

"Danette, I love you. I don't just want to touch you. I want to be with you. I want to stay with you forever."

Danette's heart opened to Laura. She too, wanted to be together forever. They were meant to be. This was right and perfect. "Laura, I love you too. We will be together forever, I know this." Danette responded to Laura's plea, pledging herself.

Before Danette had finished her confession, Laura reached out and wrapped her arms around Danette's shoulders. She kissed Danette with such passion that Danette felt her body melt onto the bed. Pulling Laura down with her, she returned the kiss with matching passion. Lying with their bodies intertwined they exchanged kiss after kiss. Their naked breasts rubbed against each other as their passion became blistering. Murmuring endearments and words of encouragement, they touched, kissed, and tasted each other's breasts until they both yearned for more. Sliding out of the rest of their clothes they explored each other's bodies. As Danette lightly touched her tongue to Laura's navel, she could feel Laura's muscles contract and a moan escaped her lips. Slowly Danette left a trail of kisses from Laura's navel lower and lower, until Danette's tongue touched Laura's folds and she could feel Laura tremble. Slowly she traced Laura's lips until they became slick with moisture. As Danette slid her tongue in and out, Laura's hips began to move about. Her hands clasped Danette's hair, holding her tightly. She murmured words of encouragement as Danette's mouth and tongue continued to intimately stroke her. Danette could feel Laura quivering, her hips moving with a rhythm all their own. As Danette continued her caressing she could hear Laura gasping her name. Laura shuddered several times, and then collapsed, as she did Danette felt her own body flood with warmth.

"Dani, please I need to hold you." Laura reached down and pulled Danette up to her. Wrapping her arms around Danette, she tightened her hold.

"I love you," she whispered as she kissed Danette deeply.

"I love you," Danette whispered back as she returned the kiss.

"Dani, I want to make love to you," Laura murmured against Danette's lips.

"I want you to, please?" Danette's voice was hoarse with passion.

Laura began to leave a trail of kisses along Danette's neck, her fingers tracing her breasts. Sliding Danette over onto her back, Laura pressed her lips against Danette's nipples and began to lightly nip with her teeth. Danette shivered with anticipation as Laura's fingertips lightly traced a path down her stomach and between her thighs. As Laura's fingers touched the wetness between her legs, Danette responded with a gasp. Danette's legs quivered as Laura stroked her, slipping her finger inside. Danette responded with a moan as Laura increased the pressure. Then Danette's hips began to twist as her body shuddered with orgasm after orgasm. Laura bent her head and her lips traced the same path as her fingers. Danette's breathing became labored as she arched her back.

"Laura!" She cried out. Laura wrapped her arms around Danette as she shivered, her breath coming in gasps. Laura slowly slid up Danette's body and pulled her tightly to her. Laura could feel Danette's heart pounding as she held her.

"Dani, you are so beautiful," Laura whispered as she nuzzled Danette's neck. "I will love you forever."

"I will love you forever." Danette pledged, still dazed with what had happened.

The two of them wrapped themselves tightly together and slowly drifted off to sleep. Love for each other blanketed them with security.

CHAPTER 7

Danette slowly woke up. She could feel the warm breath against her neck where Laura's face was pressed. Danette's arm was around her. Laura had one arm stretched around Danette's shoulders, her fingers tangled in Danette's hair. Danette could hear her heart beating softly. She looked so young lying next to Danette sound asleep. Her mouth was slightly open, with her tongue showing at the corner of her mouth. Danette's heart overflowed with feeling as she gazed at her. As if Laura knew she was being watched, her eyelashes fluttered and eyelids slowly opened. Danette continued to watch her, as Laura awakened. A slight smile came to Laura's lips as she looked back at Danette.

"Hi," She said softly.

"Hi," Danette replied with a whisper. "Did you sleep well?"

"Perfect." Laura began to stretch. "How about you?"

"Just fine." Danette answered, not quite sure how to act. Before she could say anything else, Laura slipped her body on top of Danette's. Her eyes darkened and she slid her hands down Danette's arms to her fingers. Interlinking her fingers with Danette, she bent toward her. Danette leaned upward toward Laura and their lips met, at first tentative and then with passion.

"Laura, I love you!" Danette whispered softly.

"Oh Dani, I love you too! I was so afraid that you didn't love me," Laura responded. "The whole time I was gone I thought about you. I knew I had to talk to you, to tell you how I felt, even if you didn't feel the same way. I had to take a chance." Laura's eyes watched Danette carefully.

"Laura, I felt the same way. I was scared, too! I thought something was wrong with me. I couldn't believe that I might never see you again."

"Nothing is wrong with you or me. We are meant to be together. I will never leave you. I have never felt this way before and I know I want you in my life forever." Laura began to kiss Danette on her neck. Danette's response was replaced with moans as Laura proceeded to demonstrate her love for Danette. Not much later Danette was able to express her feelings as she made love to Laura. Their lovemaking was passionate and playful as they became more familiar with each other.

Several hours later Danette and Laura were on their way over to Michael and Peter's. It had taken them much longer than usual to get ready. They couldn't seem to stop touching each other. Even in the car Laura had her hand resting on Danette's thigh.

"Laura, do you think we should tell Michael and Peter about us?"

"I'd like to tell someone. I feel so happy," Laura replied with a smile on her face.

"We have to be careful, though. If the girls in the dormitory think anything is going on they will kick us out. With our scholarships on the line, we can't afford any problems. Otherwise your parents would make you quit school. We just have to be careful!" Danette pleaded. "I couldn't stand it if we were separated."

"Dani that will never happen. We will be careful and everything will be perfect. Don't worry." She squeezed Danette's thigh to emphasize her statement.

"Okay Laura," Danette said laughing, "but if you squeeze my leg once more, we're going to get in an accident." They both had to laugh. This was all so new to them. Pulling up in front of Michael and Peter's apartment, they parked the car.

"Don't forget the Christmas presents, Danette." Danette turned the car off and Laura retrieved them from the trunk and carried them into the building. Ringing the doorbell to Michael and Peter's, Laura and Danette grinned at each other.

"Hello girls, it's about time you got here," Peter remarked as he opened the door and ushered them inside. "How come you are so late?"

"We had things to take care of." Laura responded with a grin.

"That's right." Danette chimed in, poking Laura as she walked down the hall. "We had a few things to do." She felt a little guilty telling Michael and Peter that small lie. She just didn't quite know how to tell them the truth.

"Hi sweetie, how are you?" Michael asked, hugging her. "Where's Laura?"

"I'm in the kitchen getting a pop!" Laura's voice came from the other room. Danette followed Peter into the living room along with Michael. A football game was on the television, the sound muffled. Michael and Peter made themselves comfortable on the couch and Danette sat in a chair across from them.

"Danette, do you want something to drink?" Laura yelled from the kitchen.

"Yes, please, a diet pop."

"Anyone else need anything?"

"Not a thing." Michael replied. "Get your butt out here and give me a hug."

"Here you go." Laura handed a glass of pop to Danette and set hers on the coffee table in front of the couch. She walked around to the back of the couch and wrapped her arms around both Peter and Michael. "Hi guys." They hugged her back. It was obvious how much they cared for Laura.

"Now I'm going to go sit with Danette." Laura laughed as she walked back over to Danette's chair and sat on the arm.

"Guys, we have something to talk to you about." Laura volunteered.

"You sound serious." Peter responded.

"You know you can tell us anything." Michael reassured them. "What's going on?"

"This is kind of difficult." Laura admitted, shrugging her shoulders.

"Maybe I can help." Danette interrupted. "Laura and I have realized something." As she talked, Laura reached down and took hold of her hand.

"You don't need to say another word, Danette." Michael responded, a smile on his face. "When did you two realize how you felt?"

"When I was home over Christmas I realized how I felt about Danette. When I got back we talked and she told me she felt the same way."

"We're happy for both of you." Peter grinned. "We are surprised but very happy.

Laura hugged Danette with one arm, a smile on her face. "We are happy. We are just telling the two of you and no one else. We need to be careful. If my parents ever found out they would pull me out of school. My father will only allow me to stay as long as I'm on a scholarship. If people found out we are together we both could lose our scholarships."

"With all of your father's money you would think it wouldn't matter," Peter remarked. "We won't tell anyone but I don't understand why your father would take you out of school."

"It has nothing to do with money. He thinks I am wasting my time. He wants me to marry some wealthy man of his choice and take my place in society. I can't give him any reason to even consider pulling me out now. It will give me some time to figure out how I can stay here permanently. Besides Peter, my father would never understand my wanting to be with Danette. He has no tolerance for anything other then heterosexual marriage. He would try to break Danette and I apart." While she spoke she hugged Danette tightly. "I am going to stay here. I am going to be with Danette forever."

"Don't worry Laura, we'll help you all we can." Michael vowed.

"You too Danette. Don't you worry, we'll be here for both of you." Peter pledged. "We are very happy for the two of you."

"Thanks guys, we love you both," Laura stated, as Danette shook her head in agreement. They were both so happy.

CHAPTER 8

Danette pulled into the driveway of the small house. She and Laura had rented the house midway through their sophomore year of college, and gotten part time jobs to contribute to household expenses. The two of them worked and studied hard. They both had managed to maintain almost perfect grades, insuring the continuation of their scholarships. On top of all these successes they were also celebrating their third anniversary together. They were going to celebrate on Tuesday with a small New Year's Eve party at their home. Laura's job was at a local art gallery where she also had the opportunity to show her artwork periodically. She had become quite well known in the local artist community. Her paintings easily sold when she put them on display.

She was working late tonight. Danette was going to spend some time on her new computer, a combined Christmas gift from Laura, and her aunt. She had been working part time for her aunt's company since her second year of college to contribute to their living expenses. Currently she was developing a computer software program for her final project in her business class. She had managed to take all of the required courses in business and finance to graduate with a double degree. She and Laura had both taken courses through their summer breaks. They did this for two reasons. First and foremost, they wanted to get all their requirements out of the way, and secondly, it prevented Laura from having to go back to New York over the summer. She managed to visit her family once a quarter for a week at a time but they never visited her. Laura had explained their reasons for not visiting.

"My father is too busy making money and my mother is too busy giving it away to all of her charities." She refused to let her family influence her relationship with Danette. It hurt Laura's feelings that her parents paid so little attention to her but she rarely discussed it with Danette. Danette and Laura spent most of their time with Michael and Peter and a small select group of friends. They also spent a fair amount of time with Danette's aunt and her friends. Danette, Dorothy, Michael, and Peter were the only family she needed. Laura and Danette were quite happy with their small family. Laura was hoping to be offered a teaching position with the University of Washington art department upon graduation. Her mentor and current chair in charge of the art department had approached her at the beginning of her last quarter. She had gone through a series of interviews over the past month and both Laura and Danette were praying for a job offer. This would help Laura to remain in Seattle. She needed a job right away, because they both expected her to be disowned by her parents once they heard about her relationship with Danette. She wanted to be able to tell her parents she could make it on her own. She had to. She would never leave Danette.

Danette already knew she had a job with her aunt's company once she graduated. She would start out in the accounting department. She and Laura had been planning their life together for months. They were going to save their money to buy a house of their own one day. Laura had worked on the layout and design and they had chosen colors, styles, furniture, and lighting. It would be their dream home. They loved talking about it, lying for hours in bed poring over the drawings.

They had also made plans for Laura and Peter to own their own art gallery. Peter was already working toward that goal. He currently taught art at a local high school and showed his sculptures at the same gallery Laura worked at. He saved all of his extra money towards the gallery.

Michael had found a successful position with a local software development company, which had recruited him upon graduation from college. The company was small and very innovative. All the employees including Michael spent long hours with little pay. He loved it. He had even enlisted Danette's help with some of the projects. He was still trying to recruit her to work full time upon graduation. She continued to turn him down in favor of working for her aunt, but did promise to continue to work as a consultant because she loved helping develop software.

Laura teased her unmercifully about her "obsession" with the computer. She joked that Danette would starve to death if she didn't remind her to eat. Danette had to point out to Laura that she was just as obsessed when she painted. Laura would paint for hours without a break until she got a painting exactly the way she wanted it. They both understood and respected each other's intensity. They also loved each other very much. Laura never failed to let Danette know how much she loved her. She left notes, sent cards and flowers, but most of all she showed Danette through her actions. Danette returned the feelings and made sure that Laura was safe and secure. They knew each other better than anyone. All their friends commented on how well the two of them got along. They had no reason to fight. They both had the same goals and they worked together. They also were wildly in love with each other, their relationship just got better and better. Slipping into the chair in front of her computer, Danette planned to work until Laura came home.

The telephone interrupted Danette's thoughts as she worked on a section of code.

"Hello." Danette answered, expecting it to be one of their friends.

"Hello, is Laura Benson there?" A male voice questioned.

Danette did not recognize the voice. It was a young man's voice and she knew it wasn't Laura's father. "No, I'm sorry, she's not home right now. Can I take a message?"

"Yes. Can you tell her that her cousin Devon is in town for a visit? I am staying at the Washington Athletic Club. I'm here for the weekend and would like to see her."

"I'll make sure she gets your message. Why don't you give me your telephone number?" Danette replied. She had no idea who Devon was. She would call Laura at work and give her the message.

"Thank you," The gentleman replied. As fast as he hung up, Danette dialed Laura's work number.

"Madison Gallery."

"Hello, is Laura Benson available?" Danette inquired.

"One moment please."

"Hello."

"Laura?"

"Hi Danette, how was work today?"

"Fine, Laura, hey, I just got a telephone call from your cousin Devon. He said he's in town for the weekend and would like to get together with you."

"Great, just great! Devon is here? What is he doing here? What are we going to do, Danette?" Panic could be heard in Laura's voice.

"Don't worry about it, honey, we can entertain him." Danette stated confidently. She knew they could take care of everything.

"You don't understand," Laura wailed. "If Devon is here, he's only here for one reason, to spy on me and report to my father."

"Laura, why would he do that? You haven't given your father any reason to check up on you. Let's not panic." Even as she calmed Laura, Danette felt her heart beating rapidly. She was starting to panic herself. "Laura, why don't you call him and see what he wants. Let's not get excited for nothing."

"Danette, believe me, he's here for a reason. I'll call him, though."

"Call me back, honey, okay."

"Okay, and Danette, I love you."

"I love you, too." As Laura hung up, Danette couldn't help but worry. They had been very careful, keeping their grades up and their relationship quiet. Having a relative in town could be difficult.

Danette picked up the telephone on the first ring. "Hello."

"Danette, he wants to come over to the house to visit tomorrow," Laura cried into the phone.

"Okay, I'll start cleaning right now. Is he coming for dinner?"

"Danette, I'm scared," Laura whispered into the receiver.

"Don't worry, Laura, nothing will go wrong. Do you want me to leave for the day?" Danette would do anything to make her feel better.

"No, I want you there, please?"

"I'll be here. You just hurry home tonight. We'll be ready for him, now don't worry, we'll deal with it."

As soon as she hung up the phone, Danette looked around. The house wasn't in need of heavy duty cleaning. What she needed to do was hide the pictures and cards in the bedroom. They did have two bedrooms with Laura's clothes in one room and Danette's in the other. She started in Laura's bedroom and worked her way through all the rooms, putting everything she thought she should hide in a box. She would put the box under her bed until Laura's cousin left. Two hours later as Danette finished cleaning up the kitchen the telephone rang again.

"Hello."

"Hey girl, how you doing?" It was Peter.

"Oh Peter, I'm glad you called."

"Danette, what's wrong?"

"Laura's cousin Devon is in town for a visit and Laura seems to think he's here to check up on her for her father. She's panicked."

"Danette, everything will be fine. She has one more quarter of college. Her father wouldn't pull her out of school now."

"What if he finds out about us?"

"How could he find out? You two don't act any different then anyone else. Everything will be fine, you'll see. Don't you worry."

"Okay, how about I call you tomorrow evening once this is over."

"Okay, take care Danette. Give Laura a hug, and don't worry."

"Thanks Pete, give Michael a hug."

"Will do."

Twenty minutes later Laura came bursting through the front door. "Danette, where are you?"

"Laura, I'm in the bedroom changing the sheets." She called from upstairs.

"Danette, the house looks great. What did you do with our things?" Laura asked as she entered the bedroom and threw her arms around Danette. "Boy, am I glad to see you!"

"Laura, everything's fine. The house is spotless. We'll entertain your cousin tomorrow and fix him a great dinner. I put all our stuff in a box under the bed. We will put it back out after your cousin leaves." Danette hugged Laura in return. "You just need to get a good night's sleep. Do you need to work on Sunday?"

"No, I've got the rest of the weekend off. I've got to work Monday and Tuesday night."

"You have to work on New Year's?" Danette asked, disappointment in her voice. That was the night of their small New Year's party.

"Only until seven and then I'm back here to celebrate." Laura responded to Danette's plea, and also followed it with a kiss. "I wouldn't miss our anniversary, you know that. Let's go to bed early tonight, Danette. I want to hold you and not worry about anything."

Danette had no problem with Laura's request. Tomorrow they would deal with her cousin.

CHAPTER 9

"Danette, I would like you to meet my cousin, Devon Leonard. Devon, this is my roommate Danette." Laura had opened the door to a tall slender young man with short light brown hair. He had wire rim glasses and a smile on his face.

"Hello, it's nice to meet you." He responded, reaching out to shake her hand.

"Come on in." Danette returned his handshake.

"Thanks."

"Devon, what are you doing here in Seattle? Laura inquired as they all sat down. Devon had on a blue pair of slacks, sport coat, and a tie. He looked like a very successful young executive. Danette and Laura were both wearing dress pants and sweaters. They were trying very hard not to be nervous. It was crucial that they act very natural.

"I had a little business to do in Seattle yesterday, so I thought I'd visit you while I'm here. I haven't seen you for several years. You look great Laura. It has been so long I thought we could catch up. This is a nice little house, can you show me around?"

"Sure," Laura replied with a smile. Even though Laura appeared calm, Danette could tell how nervous she was as she stood up along with Devon and herself.

"While you give Devon a tour, I'm going to work on my computer. You're staying for dinner, aren't you, Devon?"

"Why don't you let me take you both out?" He responded.

"That's all right, we have already dinner started." Laura remarked. "Come on and let me show you our home.

Danette went upstairs into what she and Laura called the workroom. It was actually another bedroom that she and Laura had turned into a half-office and half-studio. Danette's computer and printer were on one side, with a desk, a full bookshelf, and a file cabinet. The other half of the room had canvas spread on the floor, a large bulletin board on one wall, a large rolling cart, and Laura's easel. She had her current painting set up on it. She also had two tables full of paints, brushes, assorted containers, and stacks of blank canvasses leaned against the wall.

On the bulletin board were Laura's latest ideas for paintings. Her finished works were hanging on the other three walls, eight in all. Laura was preparing for her first formal one-woman show in February. She was to have ten paintings completed by then. She was working on number nine. They were overwhelming they were so good. Danette had no doubt Laura's show would be successful.

Many days and nights Laura would paint and Danette would work on her computer programming. They enjoyed working together, asking each other's opinion, and many times not speaking, just enjoying each other's company. They were each other's biggest fans. Now Danette needed to finish the computer program she was working on for her final project. It was a special database to organize employee records for her aunt's company. It would streamline their ability to respond to clients' requests for temporary services. Danette knew it would save the company lots of time and money. It would also be the last computer project required to graduate. She was very proud and excited about it.

Besides, she thought it would be better if she left Laura alone with her cousin so they could spend some time together without her. Hopefully, Laura wouldn't be quite so nervous without her around. Danette immersed herself into her work. Twenty minutes later she could hear Laura and Devon coming down the hall.

"This is our workroom," Laura remarked as she led Devon into the room. "Danette works on her computer in here and I paint."

"These are all yours?" Devon inquired as he slowly walked around the room examining the paintings on the walls.

"Yes," Laura replied shyly. It was the first time she had shown her artwork to any member of her family. Her parents repeatedly told her it was ridiculous to major in a hobby. It was hard for her to show her work to someone else who might think it was a waste of time.

"Laura, these are unbelievable! I've never seen paintings like this! Where did you find such flowers and plants to paint?" Devon exclaimed as he wandered from painting to painting. He obviously liked what he saw.

"She makes them up. It is her own special garden," Danette remarked with a smile. "You won't find them anywhere else but in her paintings. Aren't they wonderful!"

"Yes, they are beautiful!" Devon responded to Danette. "Have you shown your parents these paintings?" He continued looking. "Laura, they should see your work, you are very talented!"

"They wouldn't be interested Devon, they think my painting is a waste of time."

"They wouldn't say that if they saw your work. Your paintings are breathtaking. Anyone who looks at your work can see how good you are." Devon continued to stare at the paintings.

"She's having her first one-woman show in February at the Madison Gallery." Danette couldn't help but brag. She was glad someone from Laura's family could see how truly talented she was.

"It's no big deal." Laura face flushed red with embarrassment.

"Yes it is." Devon responded, "I'm very impressed."

"Thanks, I appreciate that."

Danette's heart warmed. She knew how important Laura's artwork was to her. As she looked at Laura, Devon wandered over to her computer.

"Talk about state of the art! Nice computer."

"Thanks." Danette grinned.

Her aunt Dorothy and Laura had given it to her for Christmas. They had worked hard to get the perfect computer. Laura had also given her a printer and she had been overwhelmed. She was still learning all of the capabilities of her new equipment.

"What are you working on?" Devon inquired. He sounded definitely interested.

"It's a database program for my aunt's company. It's to keep track of her employee records. It should make it much easier to access the information."

"How many employees?" Devon responded looking at the screen. Laura smiled as Danette sat down in front of the computer. Devon leaned over her shoulder, both of them looking intently at the computer screen.

"She has over twenty-five hundred direct employees and seven hundred temporaries that she needs to keep information on."

"And your program can handle that many?"

"Even more."

"How fast is it?" He was genuinely interested.

"Almost real time."

"Really?" Devon now sounded very impressed.

"She's something else, isn't she? You should see some of the other programs she has written." Laura loved to talk about Danette. She was proud of her.

"It's nothing," Danette said, feeling self-conscious. "Enough of this? What do you do, Devon? Laura told me you work for Laura's father?" She asked as she stood up from the computer.

"I'm a financial analyst. At least that is my title. I look over prospective companies that Laura's father is considering investing in or purchasing. He then makes a decision as to whether to invest, buy outright, or move on to another opportunity."

"That sounds interesting, how long have you been working for him?"

"Almost five years. I started right out of college and I have been working for him ever since."

"Well guys, are you hungry?" Laura interrupted. "We can continue visiting while we eat."

"I am." Devon responded.

"So am I." Danette answered.

"Well, that's a change." Laura laughed, grinning at Danette. "Come on then, let's eat."

Several hours later the three of them were sitting in the dining room laughing. It had been an enjoyable evening. They found that they had many things in common. Devon was a very nice man.

"Listen, I should get going. It's getting late and I have an early flight home." As Devon spoke he stood up. "Thanks for the dinner, I enjoyed myself."

"I'm glad you called. It's been wonderful seeing you." Laura hugged Devon good-bye.

"It was wonderful seeing you, Laura. It was nice meeting you, Danette."

"It was nice meeting you, too. Have a safe trip back."

"Thanks." Devon walked to the door with Laura trailing behind.

"Bye, Devon."

"So long Laura, good luck with your show, your paintings are fantastic!"

"Thanks." Laura shut the door behind him.

"Whew, I'm glad he's gone!" Laura sighed as she leaned against the door.

"I thought he was a nice guy," Danette responded as she slumped on the couch.

"He is a nice guy but I know he was sent here to spy on me for my father." Laura was adamant.

"Even if your father did send him, he didn't have anything to see. We were very careful, there is nothing to worry about."

"Okay, I'll stop worrying." Laura grinned at Danette.

"Worry is your middle name!"

"And you don't worry?" Laura asked as she walked toward her.

"No, not at all." Danette replied, shaking her head. She knew Laura was teasing her. She worried about everything.

As Laura reached Danette she threw her arms around her and launched herself on top of her, flattening her on to the couch. They were both glad Devon was gone.

"Dani, have I told you lately how much I love you?"

"Not for several hours." Danette grinned, wrapping her arms tightly around Laura. "I love you."

"Oh Dani, I do love you so much! Come on, let's go to bed. Everything is cleaned up." Laura stood up and took Danette's hand. They both turned out the lights and headed to their bedroom. They were once again safe in their home surrounded by their love for each other. They knew it would last forever.

It was after ten o'clock Sunday morning when the telephone rang, waking them both up.

"Hello?" Laura answered the phone, her voice groggy with sleep.

"Laura, did I wake you?" It was Danette's Aunt Dorothy.

"No Aunt Dorothy, I'm just moving slowly this morning." Danette's naked body was still wrapped around her. They had made love until late the night before and had only gotten a few hours of sleep.

"Well, I'm calling to see if I can take my two favorite girls to brunch."

"Hold on, let me go find Danette." With her hand on the mouthpiece, Laura spoke to her.

"Dani honey, it's your aunt, wake up. She wants to take us to brunch."

With a moan of impatience, Danette lifted her head up. "Do you want to go?" She asked Laura.

"Sure, why not?" Laura replied, handing her the telephone.

Clearing her voice, she took the receiver and spoke to her aunt. "Hi, Aunt Dorothy. Laura said you wanted to take us to brunch." Danette tried to sound awake.

"Yes, what do you say? We can go to "Thirteen Coins". I want to hear how the two of you are doing."

"We'd love to go. What time? Do you want us to pick you up?" Dorothy had given Danette her old car when she bought a new one. Laura and Danette shared it.

"If you don't mind?" Dorothy did not like driving in the city. "How about in one hour? Can you girls be ready by then?"

"Sure, we can. We'll see you in one hour."

"Okay honey, and Danette I'm sorry I woke the two of you up." Dorothy responded. Danette thought she heard humor in her aunt's voice. Danette hung up the phone with a puzzled look on her face.

"Dani, what's wrong?" Laura asked, watching her.

"I don't know. Do you think my aunt suspects about us?"

"Why should she, did she say something?"

"No, at least nothing about us. It was just, I don't know, the tone of her voice?" Danette replied, her own voice full of question.

"Oh Dani, I told you last night you worry too much. She doesn't know anything. What time are we picking her up?" Laura laid a quick kiss on Danette's lips.

"One hour. Who was all worried yesterday when Devon was here?"

"An hour! We had better get going. Besides your aunt is wonderful, nothing at all like my parents!" Laura exclaimed, throwing the bedcovers off the two of them. "I'll race you to the shower." She leaped off the bed already half the way to the bathroom.

"Anyone tell you, you cheat?" Danette yelled, laughing.

She did have to admit Laura was right. Her Aunt Dorothy was a terrific person. She loved Laura as much as Danette. Danette many times felt guilty not telling Dorothy about her and Laura, but she was not ready to. She knew she would eventually but she just had not found the right time.

One hour later, they pulled up in front of Dorothy's condominium. She was waiting in the front entryway. As she opened the door, she greeted them. "Good morning girls!"

Aunt Dorothy, as usual, was smartly dressed in a coordinated knit pants outfit. You never saw her when she wasn't completely put together. It was one of her traits that both Laura and Danette admired.

"Hi, Aunt Dorothy, you ready for brunch?" Danette inquired. She and Laura were much more casually dressed in jeans and sweaters.

"Of course!" Off the three of them went for a leisurely brunch at their favorite restaurant.

"So tell me how you both are doing in school?"

"Good Dorothy, Danette is going to get straight A's, as usual." Laura grinned. "I am doing very well in my classes."

"I don't doubt you both are working very hard." Dorothy smiled in return. "So have the two of you figured out what you are going to do after graduation?"

"I am still planning on starting work as soon as possible." Danette reassured her aunt. Dorothy had always planned on Danette working with her.

"Are you sure you want to do that? You have so many options available to you Danette."

"I want to work with you."

"I just want to make sure you know you have choices. Laura, aren't you and Peter still planning on your own art gallery?"

"We are, but we need to save up the money and get some gallery experience before we jump into business. He is really enjoying teaching right now."

"He makes a great teacher. How are he and Michael doing? I haven't seen them for weeks."

"They are doing well. Michael works very long hours but he loves the work. They are looking into buying a condominium in the city so we are going to help them start looking next week. They hate living in an apartment on the Eastside."

"Maybe I can help them with that. I know where several new buildings are going up and they might be smart to get into some place new."

"Thanks Aunt Dorothy."

"No problem. I like those two men very much. They are generous and loving and I consider them a member of our family."

"Dorothy, you make everyone a member of your family." Laura responded with a chuckle.

"Well, the four of you are my closest family, and I just like to see you all so happy." She patted both Danette and Laura's hands. "Now, let's talk about graduation."

They laughed and talked all morning. Aunt Dorothy was never boring. She was a unique character much loved by both Danette and Laura. After brunch, they dropped her off and then took themselves back home. Laura spent the rest of the day painting while Danette worked on her computer. Michael called later that evening to see how their dinner went with Devon and to confirm what to bring for the New Year's party. They were all looking forward to a festive evening. Danette and Laura went to bed early, anticipating a very busy week.

Monday morning came very early for Danette. She was planning to work all day to get the employee software program on line before her last quarter of school began. She needed to confirm that it worked before she wrote her final report. Arriving at the office at seven, she ran into her aunt walking into the building.

"You're here early."

"I want to finish installing the new employee software today. It will give me the rest of this week to train Denise."

Denise Johnson was the manager of Human Resources at Dorothy's company, and a partner in the planning and development of the new software. She was as excited as Danette about the installation.

"Good! Danette, you have done a great job on the project. I've only heard good things about it! I'm proud of you," Dorothy stated with a smile.

"Thanks Aunt Dorothy. I appreciate your encouragement."

"Honey, you always make me proud. I just wish your parents knew how terrific you turned out." She patted Danette on the back.

Danette blushed with pleasure as they exited the elevator. "I had better get to work." She didn't know what else to say.

"See you later, hon." Dorothy trotted off.

"Okay." Danette watched her aunt enter the lobby of her office.

She felt very lucky that her aunt was so supportive. Things could not be better in her life. Maybe she should tell her about her relationship with Laura. Danette knew she would understand. In fact, Dorothy had probably already figured it out and was waiting for Danette to talk to her. Dorothy was like that.

While Danette was beginning her day of work, Laura was busy painting. She wanted to make sure she would be ready for her show. She was proud of her paintings, and had worked hard to develop a style all her own. She was excited and honored to be having her first major show in a very respectable gallery. If it turned out to be a success it would generate some interest in her work that might help her support herself. With only one quarter to go before graduation, she had to make plans to be able to stay in Seattle. She knew once she told her parents about herself and Danette they would wash their hands of her. She turned back to her final painting, intent on her goal. She wanted to be able to make it on her own. She had to!

"It's terrific, Danette, the program is better than I thought it would be!" Denise gushed. "Do you know how much time and money this is going to save us? Your aunt is going to be so impressed. You should sell this program."

"Thanks Denise, you deserve as much credit as I do. Without your input it wouldn't have gotten done!" Danette meant her praise. Denise had worked equally as hard. She and Denise had been testing the software all afternoon and had not run into one problem. It was now five-thirty and they both were tired and excited. It had been a long day.

"We should celebrate!" Danette announced. "We could pick your kids up and go for pizza. What do you think?" Danette knew that Denise was a single parent with two children. She didn't want Denise to miss any time with them.

"That's a great idea! Why don't you call Laura? The kids haven't seen either of you for awhile. They'd enjoy it." Denise had a big smile on her face.

"I will call her," Danette responded. Denise and Laura had been instant friends from the first day they met. Laura had entertained Denise's children when she had worked with Danette.

"Hey you two, how's it going?" Aunt Dorothy popped her head in. "Denise, shouldn't you be picking up those beautiful children of yours?" Dorothy made it a point to know about her employees. She encouraged them to put their families first. She believed that a solid healthy family made a very healthy hardworking employee.

"Hi Dorothy, we're celebrating! Your niece is brilliant!" Denise grinned as Dorothy entered the office.

"I know she is." Dorothy patted Danette on the arm. "I understand from Danette that you are her partner on this software package. I take it, it was successful?"

"It is working perfectly. Danette tested it all afternoon and not one problem." Denise was a big fan of Danette's.

"Congratulations to both of you. We will make an announcement on Friday." Dorothy was insistent that her employees received credit for work well done. She held monthly company-wide meetings with the employees in the lunchroom. She shared problems and ideas, and encouraged involvement from all of her employees. They in turn provided enthusiasm and solutions to many problems. "Now did I hear the word celebration?"

"We thought we'd celebrate by going to have pizza with Denise's children. Would you like to join us?" Danette knew that Dorothy enjoyed Denise's children also.

"I'd love to, when are you going?"

"I must go pick up the kid's from the babysitter's. How about if we meet you at Luigi's in one hour?"

"Perfect!" Danette replied. "Let me call Laura and see if she wants to come. I'll bring Dorothy and we'll meet you there."

"Terrific! Now I'd better run." Denise grabbed her purse and coat and was gone.

"You call Laura and then meet me in my office. I have a few things to finish up and Danette...nice job." Dorothy grinned at Danette as she too left the office.

Danette sat there for a moment savoring the praise. They had done a good job. Everything worked on the program as planned. She couldn't wait to tell Laura.

"Hello." Laura answered the telephone.

"Hi," Danette responded softly. She loved Laura's voice.

"Hi yourself! When are you coming home? I missed you today."

"Sure, I bet you've been painting all day." Danette laughed.

"I have, but I still missed you." Laura retorted with her own chuckle. They both knew that when she painted she didn't think of anything else. She was in her own wonderfully creative world.

"Are you up to going out for pizza with Denise and her kids tonight? Aunt Dorothy will be there. It's kind of a celebration."

"The software program, did it go well?" Laura knew how hard Danette worked on it.

"Laura, it worked perfectly!" She couldn't help but boast a little.

"Oh Danette, that's fantastic! I bet your aunt is very proud of you. I know I am." Laura was very proud of Danette. She put her heart and soul into everything she did. It was one of the things Laura loved most about her. "I'd love to go!"

"Okay, we'll swing by and pick you up in about a half hour, okay? We're going to Luigi's."

"I'll be ready! Danette congratulations, I love you."

"Thanks, I love you, too!" She whispered back, and hung up the phone.

Danette had a lot to feel lucky about. Tomorrow night was their anniversary and New Year's Eve. What could be better?

CHAPTER 10

Danette surveyed the living room to make sure everything was ready for the party. Laura was on her way home and twenty of their closest friends were due in one hour. She was hoping to give Laura her anniversary present before the party began. She had chosen a beautiful antique diamond ring for Laura. They had found it at an antique store in downtown Seattle one day when they were wondering around. Laura had expressed her feelings about how much she liked it, and Danette had gone back several days later and purchased the ring. She knew Laura was going to be pleased. Now, if she would only get home in time to receive it. As Danette made one last tour around the living room she heard a car door slam. Looking out the front window, she saw Laura running up the front stairs. Laura burst through the door, a big grin on her face.

"Happy Anniversary, Dani." She threw her arms around her.

"Happy Anniversary to you. How was work tonight?" Danette inquired, kissing Laura hello.

"Surprisingly busy for New Year's Eve."

"Are you tired?" She asked, hugging her tightly.

"Not at all, I'm excited, but first I want to exchange anniversary gifts. Do we have time?"

"Just enough. I'll go get my gift."

"I've got yours right here. Danette, is there anything else to do for the party?"

"No honey, you can relax until people arrive. I think I've got everything covered." Danette answered from the other room.

"You did everything, I appreciate that."

"I know you do, Happy Anniversary, Laura." Danette slid her arms around her, handing her a small wrapped package.

"I love you, Dani." As Laura wrapped her arms around Danette, she kissed her passionately. "Do you remember our first New Year's Eve?"

"Of course I do. We exchanged Christmas gifts and went to the dance with Michael and Peter. I also remember it was the first time you kissed me." Danette smiled as she remembered. She still wore the necklace Laura had given to her.

"You kissed me first. Besides that's not all we did." Laura responded with a chuckle. "I will never forget that night. It was so special. We made love for the very first time."

"It was very special, now open your anniversary present." Danette remarked, smiling at Laura. It was three years ago and she still could remember every detail. It seemed like yesterday.

"Okay, and you open yours." Laura handed a small wooden box to Danette.

"I will, after you."

Laura's eyes sparkled as she quickly unwrapped her package. A small jeweler's box was revealed. Slowly, she lifted the lid. The light caught the diamond nestled in the center of the antique ring. Laura's hand trembled as she held the box. "Oh, it's the ring I saw in the antique store. It's beautiful, I love it Danette, thank you." She had tears in her eyes.

"Try it on and see if it fits." Danette's heart beat quickly as she watched Laura take the ring out of the box and put it on the ring finger of her left hand. It fit perfectly.

"Thank you," Laura whispered as she kissed Danette. "Thank you."

"You're welcome. I'm glad you like it."

"I love it. Now it's your turn."

Danette opened the small wooden box. It was a beautiful inlaid pattern of different types of wood. Inside, on black flannel, was a beautiful gold ring. It was in the shape of a woman with long flowing hair. The body was formed into a circle, the feet touching the head to close the circle. It was almost identical to her necklace.

"Where did you find it?" Danette asked quietly. She was stunned. It was remarkable.

"I had it made. I gave the jeweler a sketch of what I wanted. Do you like it?" Laura's voice had a trace of worry in it.

"It's fantastic, it's perfect! I can't believe you had this made, I love it! Thank you." Danette's eyes were brimming with tears as she kissed Laura. It was the most beautiful ring she had ever seen. As they stood in the middle of the living room embracing, they were interrupted by a knock on the door.

Laura looked at her watch. "We aren't expecting anyone for at least an hour, are we?" Impatience could be heard in her voice.

"It's probably Peter and Michael, they said they might come early." Danette answered as she went to get the door. Opening it wide, Danette grinned at the sight of their best friends. They both had on brilliantly colored Hawaiian shirts, flower leis, New Year's Eve paper hats, and kazoos in their mouths. As Danette watched giggling, they played an unidentifiable melody. Laura began laughing as she stood behind Danette watching their show.

"Hi guys, nice outfits," Danette commented as she let them in.

"Thank you, thank you." They both responded as they hugged Laura and Danette hello.

"These are our Happy Anniversary New Year's outfits. Don't you like?" Peter asked as he pirouetted around the living room.

"I like," Danette responded, still giggling. "The kazoos are a nice touch. I couldn't quite recognize the song, though."

"Auld Lang Syne, I think." Michael turned to her with a bow.

"Happy anniversary, girls." Peter produced a brightly wrapped package from a large bag he carried.

"Yes, open it before everyone gets here." Michael piped in.

"Danette, you open it," Laura asked, sliding an arm around her to watch. Danette removed the wrapping from a small box. Removing it, she found bright blue tissue paper surrounding a heavy object. Sliding the tissue away, she revealed a small clear sculpture of two naked women embracing, their bodies defined by a shimmering, smoke-like appearance captured with the shape.

"Oh my, this is beautiful." Laura gasped. Danette nodded her head in agreement. The sculpture was sexy and beautiful.

"Isn't it something?" Michael responded. "We found it at a small gallery in San Francisco when we were on vacation."

"Don't you think it's fantastic?" Peter remarked. "We couldn't resist buying it for the two of you."

"Thanks, you guys, we love it. We love you." Danette and Laura thanked them both with hugs and kisses.

"Let's put it on the mantle so everyone can see it."

"Good idea, Laura." Danette agreed. "Now Peter, Michael, what can I get you to drink?"

"How about if I help?" Peter linked his arm with Danette.

"Okay, come with me, sir." As she and Peter went into the kitchen, Laura and Michael sat down on the couch together. It was going to be a wonderful anniversary and New Year.

CHAPTER 11

"Laura, are you ready yet?" Danette yelled from the stairway. "You can't be late for your own show."

"I don't know what to wear!" Laura wailed from the bedroom.

"What's wrong with the clothes you have on?" Danette asked patiently. She knew Laura was nervous. She had been a basket case all week. Now she had been trying to get dressed for over an hour with no success. She was to be at the gallery in one half-hour and Danette was going to make sure she got there on time.

"I look fat," Laura responded with a whine.

"Honey, you look beautiful, I promise you." Sighing, Danette reassured her. Laura weighed one hundred pounds with all her clothes on. She didn't have an ounce of fat on her. "Come on, Laura, you know I would tell you if you didn't look great."

"Okay, I'm coming." As Laura walked down the stairs Danette watched her. She had on a simple black dress with her hair piled on top of her head in a bun she had held in place with several Japanese hair combs. She looked stunning, it took Danette's breath away.

"You look beautiful, Laura. The dress is perfect, and I love your hair." Danette smiled up at Laura as she spoke to her.

"You look pretty terrific yourself," Laura responded, smiling back. Danette had on a tan silk dress and matching jacket, her streaked blond hair was cut in a short windblown style that accentuated her large eyes.

Danette had wanted to make sure she looked good for Laura. It was her special night.

"Thank you. Now let's get in the car, please?"

"Dani, no matter what happens tonight, I appreciate all of your support." Laura wrapped her arms around Danette's neck and kissed her.

"Laura, everything is going to be perfect, you watch. Your paintings are magical. Everyone is going to love them."

"They have to," Laura whispered. She had to make sure she could support herself. Her life with Danette depended on it. Her happiness depended upon it.

"No matter what happens, we'll work it out. Remember we are forever and nothing can change that, I promise," Danette pledged kissing Laura back.

"Okay, we'd better get going." Laura seemed to be a little calmer as they left their home for the gallery. It took fifteen minutes to drive to the downtown gallery entrance.

"Laura, you had better go in while I park the car."

"What if no one shows up?" Laura whispered. She had been silent most of the drive. She had a death grip on Danette's right hand.

"You know people will be here. It's going to be okay. Now go on in, I'll be in there in just a minute." Danette spoke very calmly.

As Laura walked into the gallery, Danette's eyes followed her through the doorway. Even after three years her heart still raced as she looked at Laura. She still was the most beautiful woman Danette had ever seen. She was hoping with all her heart that Laura's showing was a total success. It was so important to her. It didn't matter if she made any money, they would be okay. Laura needed to know how good she was. This show would validate her talent.

Danette parked the car and walked into the gallery. She had seen all ten paintings Laura had finished for the show but now, as she walked through the doors, she saw them displayed for the first time. Each painting was on a separate wall with lights directed at each to enhance the bright colors. The jungle-like plants and flowers glistened as if they were alive. Danette knew in her heart that the show was going to be a perfect success!

"So, what do you think?" Laura whispered from behind her, her voice shaking with insecurity as she grasped Danette's hand.

"I think." Danette turned to face Laura, "you are going to be famous."

"You like them?"

"I love them, I always have. I'm serious, you're going to be famous."

"Thanks, I love you!" Laura smiled and quickly squeezed her hand tightly.

"I love you, too, and I know everyone is going to love your art work. Do we need to do anything to get ready?"

"No, George is making sure the champagne and hors d'oeuvres are ready."

George Madison owned and ran the Madison Gallery. He and his wife Mary had hired Laura several years earlier to work for them. They were both fans of Laura's work. He had been encouraging Laura to have a show for over two years. He was also instrumental in selling several of Laura's paintings through his gallery. He was extremely proud of her. Danette and Laura wandered into the other room and found George filling glasses with champagne.

"Hi, George, need any help?" Danette volunteered.

"Hello, Danette, thanks but I'm just finishing. Don't you look beautiful?"

"Thanks, George, you look pretty terrific yourself. Is your wife coming tonight?" George's wife Mary was another favorite of Laura and Danette. Both George and Mary were short and heavyset, outgoing, and affectionate. Having no children of their own they lavished their love and affection on their employees.

"She wouldn't miss Laura's show. She is in the back doing some paperwork. Why don't you go get her. She'd love to see you."

"I will, and George, the show looks great!"

"It does, thanks to Laura's incredible work! Go get Mary and we'll have a toast before the crowd arrives."

Danette went into the office and found Mary behind her desk, which was buried with paperwork. "Mary, come on out, it's time for a toast!" Danette smiled at her.

"Hi, Danette, don't you look beautiful." Mary pushed her glasses up on top of her head. She looked like Mrs. Claus seated behind the desk.

"George sent me to get you, it's time for a glass of champagne."

"Okay, dear. Is Laura ready for tonight?"

"She's pretty nervous, but she's ready."

"Her paintings are wonderful. I believe tonight is going to be very successful for her. Now let's go find those two." Mary placed her arm in Danette's and out they went. Laura and George were waiting for them by the food table. Behind them Danette could see several people already browsing through the gallery.

"Here you go, Danette, Mary," George remarked as he handed them a glass of champagne.

"Laura, here's to your success. Your paintings are wonderfully unique and truly fantastic." Mary lifted her glass. "May you also find happiness and true love."

"Here, here." George answered in agreement.

"Thank you," Laura replied, gazing at Danette. She had found happiness and true love.

Danette lifted her glass in acknowledgment. She knew what Laura was thinking. They were lucky they had found each other. Only one thing could make their life better and it was beginning to happen. She could see the gallery was filling up.

"Laura, look at all the people." George announced. "You had better start mingling, everyone wants to meet the artist. I'm going to saunter around myself." And off he walked.

"I'm so scared." Laura's face was pale as she looked at the crowd.

"Honey, you'll be just fine." Mary reassured her, patting her on the arm." Now you go out there and mingle." She turned Laura around and lightly pushed her toward a group of people. Laura reluctantly walked into the crowd.

"What do you think, Mary? There are quite a large number of people here. I am praying that tonight will be successful. It has to be." Danette's voice betrayed her fear.

"Now dear, have no fear, George knows what he's doing. Your Laura will be famous one day. Now you go mingle, too." Danette walked in the direction of the crowd observing their reaction to the show.

"This is fantastic stuff!"

"Have you ever seen such beautiful flowers?"

"Have you met the artist, she's a young college girl?"

As Danette wondered through the crowd she could overhear peoples' remarks. They all seemed to like what they were seeing.

"Danette." Laura came up, excitement showing on her face. "George has already sold two of the paintings, can you believe it?" Her eyes sparkled with happiness.

"See, I told you!" Danette was equally as happy. "Congratulations." They quickly hugged.

"Hey girls." Michael and Peter walked toward them both dressed in tuxedos.

"Wow, don't you two look terrific!" Laura exclaimed, kissing them both. "Well, what do you think?"

"I think you're a hit!" Michael remarked, glancing around the room.

"Laura, the show's fantastic, I always told you were talented." Peter had always been one of Laura's biggest supporters.

"I agree wholeheartedly." Danette's Aunt Dorothy joined in.

"Dorothy, I'm so glad you made it." Laura hugged her.

"I wouldn't have missed it," She replied as she returned the affection.

"Thanks for coming, Aunt Dorothy." Danette embraced her also, grateful that her aunt was so supportive of Laura.

"I'm glad to be here. Now who do I talk to about buying one of these paintings?"

"Aunt Dorothy, you don't have to do that." Laura was embarrassed.

"Of course I don't, but why wouldn't I want to own an original Laura? It's an investment." Aunt Dorothy stated adamantly.

"I'll give you one, you choose." Laura would love to give her one of her paintings.

"I won't hear of that. Now point me to the owner." Dorothy would not change her mind.

"I'll take you to George." Laura agreed, smiling. "Follow me."

As the two of them left, Danette turned to Michael and Peter. "Can you believe this? She's a hit!" She was so pleased.

"She sure is. It is wonderful. Now she can stop worrying about supporting herself." Michael reassured Danette. "Now you can stop worrying."

"I will when Laura stops worrying. You two want some champagne?"

"Sure, lead the way."

As Danette, Peter, and Michael sipped champagne and visited, Laura swiftly came up to Danette, a stricken look on her face.

"Laura, what's wrong?" Danette had never seen the look on Laura's face before.

"Danette, my parents are here!" Laura's voice choked as she spoke.

Danette was so amazed she was speechless. It took her several seconds to respond.

"Where are they?" She needed time to think.

"They're visiting with George. What are we going to do?" Laura was panicking.

"Let's go back and talk to them. Do you know why they're here?" Danette was doing her level best to remain calm. Peter and Michael were completely silent.

"I have no idea, they just walked in. Father said they were here to see the show. Something is wrong. They have never been interested in my paintings before. Why now?"

"I don't know what is going on, but we need to be friendly with them. Besides maybe they did just come to see your show and visit with you." Now Danette was beginning to panic.

"Girls, don't get excited. Laura, you go be with your parents and relax, this is an art show, nothing else. Danette, locate your Aunt Dorothy. Laura, you can introduce the two of them. Now go and don't worry. Peter and I will be around. Just act normal. Okay?" Michael spoke calmly and quietly. "Now go."

Both Laura and Danette walked quickly away, following Michael's direction.

"Why do you think they're here?" Peter asked, concern lacing his voice.

"I don't know, but I have a bad feeling about this." Michael responded looking sadly at Peter. "I hope I am wrong but I think something is up."

"Laura, this nice man was explaining how good you are at your hobby." Laura's mother smiled at her as she stood next to George. "He says you have sold all ten paintings, dear. I personally do not know what they see in these paintings of strange flowers and plants. They look a little garish to me."

Laura knew her mother would never understand her need to paint. She had also given up trying to explain to her that it wasn't a hobby. She just remained silent, the pain in her heart ignored. Glancing at Danette, she saw the smile and the slight wink. It eased her heart.

"Laura, how long do you need to remain here?" Her father's stern voice caught her attention.

"The gallery closes at ten o'clock and then I need to help clean up, Father. What do you think of the paintings?" She was hoping he would acknowledge her work.

"Very nice, Laura. Your mother and I will be staying in Seattle through tomorrow evening. Please make yourself available for breakfast. I'll have a car pick you up at nine sharp."

"Yes, Father. Can I bring Danette with me?"

"No Laura, this will just be a private family breakfast." Laura's father never changed his stern expression. Laura could not remember the last time she saw her father smile. His stern look was one she was used to seeing.

"Fine, Father, I'll be ready. Thank you for coming to my show," Laura responded. She almost shivered with nervousness.

"Hello, I'm Danette, Laura's roommate."

"Hello dear, I'm Laura's mother. I believe I've spoken to you on the phone."

"Danette, this is my Father, Victor Benson. Father, this is my roommate, Danette Johnson and her aunt Dorothy Sheppard."

"How do you do." Dorothy responded with a handshake. "You both must be so proud of your daughter. She is so talented." Dorothy spoke with enthusiasm.

Laura's father returned her handshake and nodded at Danette. "Yes, we're very proud of our daughter." He responded with no inflection in his voice.

"Would you like to celebrate your daughter's success with a glass of champagne?" George was also trying to keep things festive.

"I would like that…" Laura's mother started to remark.

"I'm sorry, we can't. I have several telephone calls to make this evening. I need to get back to the hotel." Laura's father interrupted his wife. She looked at him with a puzzled expression, but did not contradict him. "We need to get going."

"Thank you for coming, Mother and Father. I will see you in the morning."

"Yes, it was nice to meet you all," Mrs. Benson remarked, as her husband directed her toward the door.

"It was nice meeting you," Danette, Dorothy, and George all responded, as they watched the two leave the gallery. Laura's face was white with fear and shock.

"Laura, are you okay?" Danette asked, very concerned.

"Danette, something's wrong. I know it."

"Laura honey, you need to relax and celebrate your success tonight." Aunt Dorothy reassured her. "You shouldn't be worried about anything. The show was fantastic."

"Yes." George joined in. "Come on, let's go find Mary."

"George is right, let's go get Michael and Peter and celebrate. We can worry about your parents tomorrow."

Danette was concerned about Laura. She appeared to be seriously distraught. She did not want her evening ruined. It had been so successful. She gently directed Laura toward the food table where Michael and Peter were waiting. Laura started walking slowly toward them. She was still unable to shake her feeling of fear.

"Her parents weren't very friendly." Aunt Dorothy remarked quietly to Danette. "They didn't seem to be overly impressed with their only daughter's success."

"They weren't impressed, Aunt Dorothy. They don't think Laura's painting is important. Her mother calls it a hobby. Can you believe that? It is so important to Laura to paint and they don't even know it." Danette sounded very frustrated and angry.

"Danette, honey, we can't do anything about that. What we can do is make sure tonight is special for Laura, okay?" She hugged Danette as she talked. "She's part of our family, too!"

"Thanks, Aunt Dorothy, I love you."

"I love you, too, honey. Now let's go celebrate. You and Laura will be fine."

Reaching the crowd by the food table, everyone was doing their best to maintain a celebratory attitude.

"Let's make a toast," George announced. "To an up and coming artist of considerable talent." He raised his glass. "May this be the first of many successful shows." They all raised their glasses in salute. The look on Laura's face betrayed her sadness. It had been her night and now things had changed.

Forty minutes later, Danette and Laura finished cleaning up with Mary and George and they were ready to go home.

"George, I want to thank you and Mary for all your hard work. I appreciate it very much." Laura hugged them both goodbye.

"It was our pleasure, believe me. Now call me tomorrow. We need to make arrangements to get more of your paintings on display." George reminded her.

"I will."

"Honey, you and Danette get out of here. You both look exhausted." Mary shooed them both out the door.

"Goodnight, thanks again."

"You're welcome, now go home." George locked the front door behind them. Danette and Laura were silent as they walked to their car. Laura had still not said a word as Danette pulled the car into their driveway.

"Come on, Laura, let's go inside." Danette spoke softly. She locked the car and they both went inside their home. As Danette shut the door, Laura finally spoke.

"Dani, no matter what happens, I love you. Always remember that." Her voice shook with emotion.

"Laura, honey, what's going on?" Danette hugged her tightly. "I know you love me, there's nothing to worry about. You just sold ten paintings at your first show. You should be excited and happy. Things couldn't be better."

"Danette, I know my parents are here for a reason. I know my father is up to something." Laura's voice was full of panic.

"Honey, you are just tired, you've had a very busy day. Let's just go to bed, things will look better in the morning, I promise." She led Laura up the stairs to their bedroom.

CHAPTER 12

The alarm went off at seven, waking Danette up from a sound sleep. She rolled over and looked at Laura as she continued to sleep. Laura had her hair pulled back into a loose braid. Unable to relax after they had gone to bed, she had tossed and turned for several hours before she finally fell asleep. Danette could watch her sleep all day, but she knew Laura was to have breakfast with her parents at nine.

"Laura, wake up, it's seven o'clock. Come on, honey it's time to get up." She moved closer, whispering softly to her. In response, Laura moved her body closer to Danette, sliding her arms around her neck and pulling her close.

Slowly her eyes fluttered open and she smiled. "Good morning." She answered, her voice husky with sleep.

"Good morning, how did you sleep?"

"Restless."

"Listen, you need to get up, you have breakfast with your parents this morning." Danette reminded her.

"We have time." Laura responded, sliding on top of Danette. Her hands slipped under Danette's nightshirt, pushing it up.

"Laura," Danette gasped, she couldn't help but respond. Laura and Danette made love with an intensity that was blinding. It was quite awhile before either of them looked at the clock.

"Laura, you had better get going." They both were lying there enjoying the lethargy that overtook them. Wrapped around each other, they were comfortable and safe in their familiarity.

"I know, just ten more minutes please?" Laura pleaded.

"You're the one who has to be somewhere," Danette replied. She, too, wanted to prolong their getting up as long as possible.

Ten minutes later, Laura slowly got out of bed. "What are you going to do today?" She asked as she selected clothes from her closet.

"I'm going into work this morning and do a little paperwork. I'll be home around four o'clock."

"Great, I should be home from breakfast about noon. I think I'll get some painting in."

Danette got up as Laura stepped into the shower. A half hour later Laura was on her way out the door. Giving Danette a hug and kiss good-bye, she was gone.

Danette took her time getting ready for work. She would probably be the only one in the building, which was fine with her. She needed to get some uninterrupted paperwork done. She would not have much time in the next month for work. She had one quarter of college left before graduation. She and Laura had both attended summer classes and would both be able to graduate with their degrees in June, a full year ahead of schedule. They had worked very hard and it was almost over. She sighed as finished her cup of coffee and left. All the hard work was worth it if she and Laura were together.

Danette had been hard at work since ten thirty and it was now two thirty. She had tried to call Laura at home twice with no answer. Assuming she must have decided to visit longer with her parents, Danette was going to finish and head home. She was exhausted and she was sure Laura was equally as tired. She planned on fixing an early dinner and going to bed. She closed her office door and headed down the hall. As she reached the elevator, it opened to reveal her Aunt Dorothy.

"Danette, what are you doing here?"

"Finishing some paperwork, Aunt Dorothy. I was just leaving. What are you doing here?"

"I had to pick up some papers I left on my desk. Why don't you wait one minute and I'll walk with you?"

"Okay." It took ten minutes for Dorothy to return. Danette was becoming anxious about getting home.

"How is Laura doing? She had a pretty busy night." Dorothy inquired.

"She's pretty exhausted. She is also pretty stressed out about her parents being here. She seems to think her father is up to something." Danette revealed to Dorothy. "He sure was cold last night."

"I wish they both had been more enthusiastic about Laura's artwork. She has a wonderful career ahead of her." Dorothy responded. "She worked hard to get through college and develop her talent, they should acknowledge that."

"Aunt Dorothy, I love you. You are always so encouraging. I know Laura appreciates your support. Thank you."

"Honey, I love Laura, the two of you are like my daughters. I am very proud of you both. I couldn't ask for two more responsible people. I think the two of you are perfect together."

Danette was so caught off guard by the remark she didn't respond. She just listened as Dorothy continued to speak. "It isn't often that two people find the sort of love that the two of you have for each other. It is very special."

"Thank you, Aunt Dorothy, I don't know what to say." Danette's eyes were filled with tears.

"Honey, there is nothing to say. Now tell me what Laura does now that she has sold all of her paintings." Dorothy hugged her obviously surprised niece.

As they conversed, they walked through the building to their parked cars. "Danette, you go home and give Laura a hug for me." Dorothy hugged Danette good-bye and they both drove home.

Twenty minutes later Danette pulled into her driveway. She was feeling incredibly tired but excited to tell Laura what her Aunt Dorothy had said. She felt very lucky at that moment. She knew Laura was even more exhausted then her. She was hoping Laura was already home and relaxing. Telling her what Dorothy had said would make her much happier.

Opening the front door, she immediately noticed that some small pictures of her and Laura were missing from the mantle. She looked around, puzzled. Something was wrong. She called out Laura's name. Upon getting no answer, she quickly ran up the stairs. Entering the bedroom that she and Laura shared, she stopped short. The closet doors were open and Laura's clothes were gone. The dresser drawers were pulled out and empty. The first thought that crossed Danette's mind was that they had been robbed. She quickly went to the other bedroom where she kept her clothes. As she walked through the door, she noticed an envelope propped up on top of her dresser. Her name was written on the front in Laura's handwriting. Danette's heart jumped immediately to her throat. Only Laura's things were gone. She picked up the envelope and hesitated, her hands quaking with fear. She slid the single piece of paper from the envelope. Taking a deep breath, Danette began to read.

"Dear Danette, I hope you will understand what I am writing to you. I must leave Seattle and you. I tried very hard to make it work but it is just too hard. I have only taken my clothes and personal things. Please know that I will love you forever. You will always be in my heart. I will not contact you, and please don't try to contact me. I have made up my mind this is best for both of us. I am sorry I couldn't tell you in person. Please say good-bye to Aunt Dorothy, Michael, and Peter. I will miss you all very much. Danette thank you for everything. You taught me what true love is. Thank you. I love you and I'm sorry, Laura." Danette was stunned. She had to re-read the note twice.

She sat on the bed staring at the paper, the words blurring before her eyes. This has to be a mistake. She and Laura had made plans. Laura had just had a successful art show, why would she leave? Something was very wrong. Danette was so shocked she had no idea what to do. She just sat there in silence. The telephone ringing in the background finally broke through her stupor. She slowly got up and answered it.

"Hello." Danette could barely get a whisper from her throat.

"Is that you, Danette?" Michael asked. "Are you okay?"

"No." Danette could barely get that one word out of her mouth. She just couldn't seem to think. Everything was all mixed up.

"Danette, what's wrong?"

"She's gone, Michael. Laura's gone."

"What do you mean, she's gone?" Michael sounded shocked.

"She's gone, she left a note." Danette still could not believe what she was saying.

"Honey, Peter and I will be right there. Don't you do anything, please."

"Okay." Even after Michael had hung up she stood there with the receiver in her hand for several minutes. She couldn't decide what to do next. Slowly, she wandered downstairs. She would make some coffee for Michael and Peter. She had nothing else to do.

"Danette, where are you?" Peter yelled as he opened the front door.

"In the kitchen."

Michael and Peter burst through the kitchen entryway. "Danette, what are you doing?" Michael asked, watching her closely.

"Making coffee," She replied.

Peter and Michael both watched as Danette tried to measure the coffee. Her hands shook so bad she couldn't fill the scoop.

"Here, let me do that." Peter suggested softly, slowly taking the scoop out of her hand.

"She left a note." Danette stated, no emotion in her voice.

Michael led Danette out of the kitchen and gently lowered her onto the couch. Worry showed on Michael's face. Danette was obviously in shock.

"May I see the note?" Michael asked slowly.

"Yes." She handed the crumpled piece of paper to him. "She took all her clothes and some pictures and left." Danette's voice cracked as she spoke. "She just left a note." Tears had begun to slide down her face. Michael put the note aside and wrapped his arms around Danette. He sat on the couch and gathered Danette up and pulled her onto his lap. He rocked her gently as she cried. Michael cried with her as he held her trying to console her.

Peter came out of the kitchen and sat on the chair across from them. He read the note Laura left and was as shocked as Danette. He certainly didn't understand why Laura had left. She had no reason to leave. He knew she loved Danette there was no question in his mind. It did not make any sense. His heart broke as he watched Michael try to comfort Danette. Peter couldn't prevent the tears from rolling down his face. His best friend was broken hearted and he could do nothing to help her.

CHAPTER 13

The telephone interrupted Danette's memories, as Cindi's voice brought her back to the present. She had a meeting in one hour. She pushed her memories into the back of her mind where they belonged.

For two months Danette had prepared herself for her face-to-face meeting with Laura's daughter, but she was still hesitant as she walked into Denise Johnson's office. It was Carole's first day of work. She and her new husband had moved into the rental house two weeks earlier and gotten settled. John had taken care of all the arrangements and he had assured Danette that the couple loved the house. Carole had arrived at seven-thirty but Danette had waited until nine o'clock before she went downstairs to meet her.

Denise was seated at her desk, and sitting across from Denise was a slender dark-haired woman. From the back, she looked just like Laura did when she was in college. Her hair was in a single braid down the middle of her back. Danette's breath caught in her throat as Carole turned to look at her. Her heart beat rapidly as she looked directly at Laura's daughter. For a moment Danette could only stare. Carole looked so much like her mother.

Denise's voice captured her attention. "Danette, this is Carole Capoletti. Carole, this is Danette Johnson, chief executive officer and our fearless leader."

"Hello, it's nice to meet you." Carole's voice was not as husky as Danette remembered Laura's voice was. Carole stood up and reached out to shake hands.

"Hello, welcome to the Sheppard Corporation," Danette replied with a smile, reaching out to return the handshake. Carole was much taller than Laura, almost as tall as Danette.

"Thank you, I'm looking forward to working here."

"Good, I've heard nothing but good things from Denise about you. We need good people."

"Thank you again." Carole seemed to be embarrassed as she started to blush. Danette couldn't help but grin as she remembered that Laura used to blush heavily when she got embarrassed.

"I understand congratulations are in order, being a newlywed and all."

Carole turned bright red. "It's hard to believe it's only been three weeks. So much has happened so quickly." She smiled as she responded.

Danette's heart skipped a beat as she saw Laura's likeness in Carole's face. "Well, I had better let the two of you get back to work," Danette remarked. "Denise, I'll see you later at the management meeting. It was nice to meet you, Carole."

"Right Danette, thanks for stopping by."

"You bet." As Danette left the office, she could finally breathe more easily. It would take her a while to get used to seeing Carole around the office.

After Danette left the office, Carole turned back toward Denise. She had a puzzled look on her face. "She's very young, isn't she?" Carole asked.

"She's forty-three years old, she just looks a lot younger than she is." Denise replied. "She's one of the sharpest people I've ever met. So was her Aunt Dorothy, the original founder of the company. Dorothy was both honest and generous to a fault, and Danette is just like her. I've been working here close to thirty years and I wouldn't want to be anywhere else."

"She's the same age as my mother," Carole remarked. "My mother went to the University of Washington for three years until she got married. She's the reason my husband and I came here."

"Danette graduated from the University of Washington. What a coincidence." Denise remarked. She knew who Carole's mother was but Denise would not intrude on Danette's privacy. She loved her too much.

"Yes, it sure is." Carole stated, as she seemed to be considering something very important. "You had better show me something to get started on. You have a meeting coming up."

"You're right, we had better get started." Denise and Carole both settled into their chairs and began to work.

Four months later found Carole not only settled into her job but also developing a fast reputation for being efficient, highly competent, and a very pleasant person to work with. She had become instantly invaluable to Denise, who congratulated herself daily for hiring her. Carole had also become an immediate friend of Cindi's despite the differences in their background. They ate lunch, took breaks, and had even begun to work out together after work. Cindi and her girlfriend, Susan had Carole and her husband Tony over to their home for dinner several times. The four of them had gotten along famously.

Today Carole and Cindi were going to have lunch in Danette's office. Danette was out of town for several days, meeting with a client in Los Angeles. Cindi did not want to leave the office because she was expecting Danette to call in.

"Cindi, are you ready to eat?" Carole asked as she walked through Cindi's office door, carrying a large paper bag.

"Yep, I'm ready, let's go into Danette's office. The view is fantastic!"

"I've never been in her office before," Carole responded. "She won't mind?"

"Not at all, she knows I eat lunch in her office when she's gone. It's quiet and much more private than the lunchroom." As Cindi responded she led the way through double doors into Danette's office. The first thing Carole noticed were the two full floor-to-ceiling windows. Since it was a corner office that faced west, there was a perfect view of the waterfront and Puget Sound. The other window faced north, which afforded a view of Pike Place Market and the north end of Seattle. It was spectacular.

"You're right the view is fantastic!" Carole stated enthusiastically. "I don't know how Danette can concentrate on work with this view. I couldn't." As she spoke she turned around to where Cindi was standing. The wall directly behind Cindi was full of shelves with lighted recessed areas displaying different pieces of art. She stepped closer to look.

"What a wonderful collection of art!" She remarked as she moved from one piece to the other.

"Danette's Aunt Dorothy was very active in the artist community when she was alive. She and Danette have both helped young artists get their start. It is quite a collection."

Carole turned to the last wall, which had the double entry doors. On either side was a collection of framed photographs, most of them from special company events over the years. Carole stepped up to one photograph in order to see it clearly.

"That is a picture of Dorothy Sheppard at the company Christmas party. That was a year before she passed away," Cindi remarked. "She always had a wonderful party at her home. Danette still carries on the tradition every Christmas eve."

As Carole looked at the picture, she gasped, "That's a painting of my mother's!" Sure enough, behind the figure of Dorothy and several employees, on the far wall of Dorothy's condominium, was one of Laura's paintings. Carole could recognize it because it was almost identical to the paintings she had done while Carole was growing up. They were unique in style.

Cindi remained silent, not sure what to say in response. She had forgotten about Laura's painting in the picture.

"I'm sure that's my mother's work, her style is very different, but why would Dorothy Sheppard have a painting of my mother's? She just started painting again since grandfather died. He would not allow it in his home. She used to paint when I was younger." Carole's grandfather had passed away not two weeks after she and her husband moved to Seattle.

"Mother had stopped painting when father died and we moved in with grandfather. He never did approve of mother's painting. She was an art major in college while she was here at the University. She absolutely loves to paint." The puzzlement could be heard in Carole's voice.

"I'll bet she was one of the artists Dorothy helped out." Cindi hoped her explanation made sense. She didn't want Carole to ask any more questions.

"Wouldn't that be a small world," Carole responded with a smile. " Let's eat."

Cindi breathed a silent sigh of relief. Carole seemed to have accepted her explanation. "Let's do that."

They both walked to the circular conference table and prepared to eat their lunch. They began discussing the upcoming company party, since Carole was chairperson and Cindi was one of the committee members they had a lot to talk about. Cindi assumed the painting was forgotten. It was not.

"Cindi, I have a surprise to tell you." Carole grinned, her eyes sparkling.

"What's up, that good looking husband of yours getting straight A's again?" Cindi teased her. Tony was not only a handsome man, and a very talented student; he was also one of the nicest men Cindi had ever met.

"Of course, but that's not my secret," Carole quipped back. "I'm pregnant."

"Congratulations, Carole." Cindi knew that Tony and Carole wanted a child. "That's fantastic, when is the baby due?" Cindi gave Carole a big hug.

"Sometime toward the end of next July," Carole responded hugging her back.

"I bet Tony is excited."

"Oh, Cindi, he's already planning the baby's room." Carole laughed.

"Does he want a boy?"

"I don't think it matters to him, he just loves kids."

"Tell Tony congratulations and tell him Susan and I will baby-sit any time."

"I will, I called my mother last night and told her. She's going to come out and help when I get closer to my due date."

"That would be wonderful, I know how close the two of you are." Cindi couldn't help but get a little worried. What if Carole's mother and Danette ran into each other? What would that do to Danette? Cindi would hate to see Danette hurt in any way.

"What does your mother do, Carole?" Cindi was curious about Laura.

"She works several days a week at a homeless shelter and spends one day a week volunteering at the local hospital. She used to take care of grandfather until he passed away. Now the rest of her time is spent creating wonderful paintings." As Carole spoke about her mother, she had a smile on her face.

"You miss her." Cindi responded.

"She's my best friend, I can talk to her about anything. You would like her, Cindi."

"She sounds wonderful." Cindi felt guilty pumping Carole for information. "I'd like to meet her. What does she look like?"

"Here, I have a picture of her." Carole pulled her wallet from her purse and extracted a photograph. After looking at it for a moment, she handed it to Cindi.

Cindi looked at the picture. Laura certainly didn't look old enough to be Carole's mother. She was stunning. She looked almost identical to the photograph Danette had of her. "She is beautiful Carole, you could be sisters." She remarked sincerely as she handed it back to Carole.

"She is gorgeous, but what makes her so special is she's such a wonderful person. She took care of Father when he became ill, she took care of her mother when she became sick, and after that she took care of grandfather when he had his stroke. You know I never have heard her complain once," Carole remarked.

"In fact, the only time I have ever seen my mother get angry was when my grandfather tried to prevent my marrying Tony. They were in grandfather's study and I heard my mother's voice. Her voice was raised in anger and she was speaking to my grandfather. I remember what she said so clearly." Carole closed her eyes as she repeated from memory what she had heard.

'You may have been able to control my life but you will not ruin my daughter's. She is going to marry Tony and you will do nothing to stop it. If you try to do anything I will let some of your business acquaintances know how you managed to be so successful. I'm sure they would find blackmail interesting."

"I won't give her any of my money, I will disown her if she marries that low life."

"Fine, Father, she doesn't need any of your money. She will have her own when she turns twenty-five. She will receive the trust fund her father set up. Besides, Father, as you well know, Carole doesn't see money as the source of happiness." Laura stated proudly.

"That is your doing, you corrupted her." He accused.

"Yes, it is my fault. I will take full credit for teaching my daughter healthy values. She has fallen in love with a wonderful man whom I approve of. He is hard working, loyal, and thoughtful, and he is madly in love with Carole."

"Love, what is love! He will never amount to anything. He comes from nothing!"

"You're wrong, Father, he comes from a loving, wonderful family, unlike ours. He will provide for Carole and their love for one another will be enough."

"What did love do for you, daughter?" The sarcasm dripped from his voice as he spoke. "A sordid immoral relationship. If it wasn't for me, your life would be ruined. I saved you from yourself."

"What you did, Father, was ruin my life and threaten to ruin the lives of the people I loved most."

"If it wasn't for me, you wouldn't have had Carole. At this statement there was dead silence for several moments and then my mother responded so quietly that I could barely hear her."

'Your right, Father, she is the one perfect thing in my life. Thank you for that. Do not attempt to hurt her or prevent her wedding. I am not threatening to tell your business partners, it is a promise."

"I left the hallway then, because my mother came out of grandfather's den. All I know is that he didn't interfere with the wedding plans from that day on. He just ignored everything and did not attend the wedding. I never questioned my mother about what I heard. I wish I had." Carole remarked sadly.

" I know my mother cared for my father but I knew she was never in love with him. You could tell by the way they treated each other. It was like they were acquaintances. He was twenty-eight years older than she was. I remember hearing my cousins talking about my parents when I was very young, something about an arranged marriage to save my mother from scandal. Crazy story, huh?"

"Not so crazy, Carole. Maybe you just need to ask your mother to tell you the truth. She sounds like someone who would tell you if you asked." Cindi couldn't help but feel she was betraying Carole. She knew what the scandal was. It broke her heart to hear how much pain and heartache Danette and now Laura had suffered.

"You know, Cindi, I just might do that. What I never understood is why my mother never dated after my father passed away. She had many nice men ask her out but she never went." Carole's face revealed her puzzlement. "You would think after an arranged marriage that she would want to find someone to really fall in love with. She deserves to."

"Maybe she's still in love with the per... uh man she had an affair with. You know what everyone says. First love, forever love." Cindi tried to respond lightheartedly.

"Oh, Cindi, wouldn't that be something! If my mother could find the man she first fell in love with, she could be happy again. Maybe I can figure out who it was and get them back together. I would love to see my mother fall in love. She deserves to be loved."

"Carole, enough of this fantasy love talk, we've got work to do on this picnic." Cindi needed to change the subject before Carole continued her discussion of her mother. Cindi was becoming extremely uncomfortable, knowing the true story. She needed to get back on safe ground. Besides Carole would not take much encouragement to pursue a stunt like that. She was always looking for ways to make people happy. Something like that would appeal to her especially with her mother. Carole loved her mother very much. Cindi was a little nervous about the whole situation. It could backfire and cause a lot of heartache. She needed to make sure that Carole didn't attempt to do anything that might hurt Laura or Danette. They had enough heartbreak in their lives.

"Cindi, here's the list of food for the company party, do you think this will be enough?" Carole asked, changing the subject. "And Cindi, thanks for listening."

"No problem. What are best friends for?" Cindi smiled as she responded. She breathed a sigh of relief as she looked at the list. "This looks like plenty of food." As she and Carole discussed other details for the picnic until the end of their lunch, Cindi thought the discussion of Carole's mother had ended. Cindi was very wrong.

Three nights later, as Cindi and Susan were enjoying a quiet night together, the telephone rang. After answering the telephone Susan handed it to Cindi.

"It's Carole. She sounds upset."

"Carole, this is Cindi, what's up?"

"Cindi, can I come over and talk to you?" Susan was right. Carole sounded very upset.

"Carole, honey, what's wrong? Are you okay? Is Tony okay?"

"We're both fine, it's nothing like that. I need to talk to you about my mother."

Cindi's heart skipped a beat. "Is she okay?"

"She's fine, Cindi. I'll explain when I get there." Carole sounded very keyed up.

"Wait, Carole, I'll come over there. I can get to your place in fifteen minutes. Okay?"

"All right, Cindi. Thanks. This is really important."

As Cindi hung up the phone, she turned to Susan. "I'm going over to Carole's. She is extremely upset. It has something to do with her mother."

"She's not hurt or ill, is she?" Susan asked with concern.

"No, it's not anything like that, Susan, but something has definitely upset Carole."

"You better hurry over there. You let me know if I can do anything to help."

"I will, honey, love you. I don't think I'll be too late. I'll call if it looks like I'll be there after ten."

"Okay, love you, too, be careful driving."

"I will," Cindi promised as she grabbed a jacket and her purse. She knew that tonight something important was happening, she just wasn't sure what. Ten minutes later, as she pulled up in front of Carole's house, she could see her in the window. Cindi hurried up the walkway, impatient to know what was upsetting Carole. The door opened as she reached it.

"Carole, what is it?" Cindi saw the serious intense look on Carole's face. "Is Tony here?"

"No, he's at class. He won't be home until after ten-thirty. Cindi, come in and sit down, I have something to show you." As Carole talked, Cindi noticed she had a photograph in her hand. On the floor of the living room were other photographs and a photo album.

"I was putting some new pictures in our photo album and started looking back at some old pictures of my mother and father." Carole paced as she spoke, the photograph still clutched in her hand.

"Carole, sit down, you are making me nervous." Cindi pleaded, still unable to understand what had her so upset.

"Cindi, listen to me, this is very important. Many years ago, I believe I was seven or eight at the time, I was in my mother's room playing with her jewelry. I found some photographs in the bottom of her jewelry box. They were from when she was in college. I remember her showing them to me and putting them away. There was one I particularly liked of my mother. One day while she was gone from the house, I went to her jewelry box and took the picture. I carried it around with me for a while and then hid it in my room. Several years later, I found the picture and saved it in my diary."

Cindi was seated silent on the couch, she knew who was in the picture without being told. She was hoping Carole was not too angry with her mother and Danette.

"When I got married I threw all my old treasures and things in a box. I was going to go through them after we were settled. Tonight I went through my things, and this is what I found." As Carole finished speaking, she slowly handed the photograph to Cindi.

Afraid to look, Cindi momentarily closed her eyes. As she opened them her thoughts were confirmed. In the photograph was a young

Laura identical to the photograph Danette had shown to her. Standing next to her was a very young Danette. They had their arms casually around each other and the expression on both of their faces was one of complete happiness and love. It was very obvious to anyone who looked at the picture. Preparing herself to respond to Carole's reaction, she waited for Carole to continue. She wasn't sure how she should respond.

"I can't believe what my grandfather did to my mother, just because she was in love with another woman. Especially one as special as Danette." Carole had become as loyal to Danette as Cindi.

Cindi was surprised. She still didn't respond, as Carole continued.

"He forced her to marry my father. I know he did. She left college one month before she graduated. When I found out I never understood why she left so close to graduation, but now I do. My grandfather must have forced her. How could he be so cruel?" Carole was so upset she had begun to cry.

"Carole, calm down, you need to remember the baby." Cindi took Carole's arm and led her to a chair. "Please sit down and let's talk calmly."

Carole heeded her advice and sat down, looking up at Cindi. Tears were still rolling down her cheeks. "Why would my grandfather be so cruel?" She spoke so softly Cindi could barely hear her.

Cindi knelt down in front of Carole and took both of her hands. "Carole, you know how hard your grandfather tried to stop you from marrying Tony. Imagine over twenty years ago his finding out that his only daughter was in love with another woman. He must have been very angry. Even now, a lot of parents disown their children when they tell them they are gay." She spoke very quietly in hopes that Carole would calm down.

"I can't believe parents would be that cruel to their own children." Carole had stopped crying, and spoke in response to Cindi's words. "It wouldn't matter to my mother and it wouldn't matter to me."

"Carole, honey, not all people are as enlightened as you are." Cindi continued to hold Carole's hands. "You are lucky that you were brought up like you were. Susan's parents have not spoken to her in over three years, since she told them she was gay. They are ashamed of her, a brilliant engineer, a beautiful person, and their oldest child. It broke her heart."

"That is so sad!" Carole responded. "I'm so sorry." Tears threatened to begin again.

"Honey, it's not your fault. Now, we need to talk about the picture you found. I need to fill you in on a little information." Cindi was hoping Carole would not get angry with her.

"You mean you knew about this?"

"Yes, I have known for several years about Laura and Danette, but I think you need to hear the whole story." Cindi stood up and began pacing as she spoke. Carole remained silent as Cindi began her story.

"Your mother and Danette met their first week of college. According to Michael and Peter, who were their best friends, they were inseparable. They stayed together for over three years and were making plans to graduate and live with each other. They had pledged to be together forever. It was a shock to Peter and Michael when Laura left. She didn't explain it to any of them but left a handwritten note for Danette. It was the day after your mother had a very successful art show. They have not seen each other or spoken since that day."

Cindi continued to pace, and Carole remained silent in her chair. "Michael flew to New York to speak to your mother about two weeks after she left and she did see him. She told him she was getting married to your father. She also asked him to tell Danette she would always love her, but she was doing what she wanted to do. Several weeks later, she was married."

"My God, Cindi, my grandfather forced her to marry. He must have threatened her with something! I know my mother. She would not have left Danette without a good reason. Something or someone forced her to leave. I know she wouldn't have left on her own. It is so sad."

"Yes, it is. It broke Danette's heart. She has not really been with anyone seriously since then," Cindi revealed.

"She must have loved my mother very much. You know, Cindi, I can see why my mother loved Danette. She is always so generous and fair to everyone and she is very beautiful."

"She's just like her Aunt Dorothy, generous to a fault. And yes, she is gorgeous."

"Cindi, no wonder my mother has never dated. After being forced into a marriage she did not want, I imagine being left alone would have been a relief."

"Carole, your mother received one gift from her marriage to your father," Cindi responded.

"What's that?" Carole inquired, a puzzled look on her face.

"She would probably tell you she received the greatest gift of all, you."

"Oh, Cindi, she is a wonderful mother. I am so lucky. I just wish she could have been loved all her life like Tony loves me."

"Carole, she is loved. Let me tell you the rest of the story. From the day Laura left, Danette has loved her more than she will ever know." Cindi told Carole how Danette had privately made sure Laura was okay. When she got to the part about Tony's scholarship and the rental house, Carole had begun to cry again.

"I can't believe that she would take care of us after my mother left her with no explanation. She must still love her to do all this." She sobbed.

"Carole, you have got to stop crying. It's not good for you and the baby. Tony would be furious if he saw you," Cindi stated, knowing how much he worried about his young wife.

"Cindi, I can't tell Tony about the scholarship or the house. He is funny about things like that. He wants us to make it on our own. Oh my, that is why I was given the job. Danette gave it to me. I'm so embarrassed."

"No, that's not true, Carole. Danette asked if we had any positions open that you could fill. It was Denise who decided to hire you because of your skills." Cindi reassured her. "Besides, can you imagine how difficult it was for Danette to see you at the office? You look a lot like your mother and she sees you almost every day. Every time she sees you she is reminded of Laura."

"I didn't think of that, Cindi. It must be very hard for her. This whole story is unbelievable."

"Yes, it is." Cindi agreed, as she slumped onto the couch. "Now, you need to forget this whole thing and act like you know nothing. If Danette ever found out I told you all of this, she would never forgive me."

"I can't forget any of this, but Danette will never find out I know anything. I am going to talk to Mother about this some day, as soon as I figure out how," Carole promised.

"It is some kind of tale," Cindi stated with a smile on her face. "A true love story."

"It's a wonderful love story, but it needs a happy ending." Carole responded with a smile on her face. Her eyes had begun to twinkle.

"Now Carole, I know you. What are you cooking up in that pretty head of yours?" Cindi inquired, grinning at Carole. She had helped Carole several times on her mini-schemes. One was a surprise birthday party for Denise Johnson and another involved a blind date for a young man who worked with Carole. Cindi knew she was planning something.

"Cindi, wouldn't it be wonderful if my mother and Danette could be reunited after all these years?"

"Carole, don't even think like that. It has been over twenty years. They have both changed considerably. Besides, you promised you wouldn't tell anyone."

"I'll keep my promise Cindi, except I have to tell Tony." She grinned at her. "I promise I won't tell anyone else."

"Carole, I mean it, no schemes." Cindi demanded.

"Okay, okay."

Cindi still did not quite believe her. After visiting for twenty more minutes, Cindi hugged Carole good-bye and left for home. Upon arriving there, she updated a worried Susan as to what had happened. They discussed it as they prepared for bed.

"Susan, it was strange. Here I was expecting Carole to be angry with her mother over her relationship with Danette, but she was furious with her grandfather. She knew Laura would not have left on her own. You know, Susan, I think she is right. I believe her grandfather threatened to harm Danette somehow. Carole was insistent that Laura wouldn't have left on her own."

"What could he have done? He was a business man, not a mobster," Susan responded as she folded the quilt on their bed. "Didn't you tell me he was very wealthy?"

"Yes, that's what Danette said." Cindi stated as she crawled into bed.

"Maybe that's how he threatened Laura. He threatened to harm Danette's aunt's company. He could have done that," Susan speculated as she too slid under the covers.

"You know, Susan, I bet you are right! Carole overheard her mother and grandfather argue one night. She said Laura told him she would not allow him to ruin Carole's life like he had done to hers. I bet you are right. We are so lucky to have found each other. I cannot believe this whole story. It is amazing." Cindi remarked as she wrapped her arms around Susan.

"We are very lucky," Susan agreed, as she hugged Cindi to her. They were both very happy and very lucky.

CHAPTER 14

The telephone rang on Cindi's desk. "What now?" She thought as she picked up the receiver. It wasn't even lunch yet, but she was exhausted. She was having a very busy morning.

"Hello. Cindi speaking."

"Hi, can you get away for a quick lunch?" It was Carole.

"Yes, but it will have to be short, I'm swamped today."

"So am I. How about we eat in my office. I'll run downstairs and pick up a couple of salads."

"Sounds good, I'll be there at noon."

"Great, see you then."

"So, are you having as bad a day as I am?" Cindi asked as she walked into Carole's office.

"It's been a crazy morning. I needed a break," Carole responded. "Have a seat. Here is your salad. I also got you a lemonade."

"Terrific, thank you, what do I owe you?"

"You pay the next time."

"You got it!"

"I told Tony last night." Carole remarked as she began to eat her lunch.

"What was his reaction?" Cindi inquired, curiosity in her voice.

"It made him sad. He agreed with me that I should talk to my mother about it. He thought my mother would like to know that I love her for who she is."

"I'm sure she would, Carole." Cindi responded with a smile. "When are you going to talk to her?"

"I don't know. I would rather not do it over the telephone. I thought I would wait until she comes to help with the baby. She's planning to arrive sometime in early July."

"I think it should be in person," Cindi agreed. "I told Susan last night."

"What did she say?"

"She thought you were right when you suspected your grandfather of forcing your mother into marriage. She suggested that he might have threatened to hurt Danette's aunt's business."

"That's what Tony thought. He agreed that threatening Danette or her aunt would be the only reason mom would have left. The night before my wedding, my mother and I had a long talk. It is now making sense to me. She told me that true love happens once in a person's lifetime and you should do whatever it takes to nurture and protect it. I thought she was talking about Tony and myself, but now I know it was what she had done. She had protected her own true love. I know she didn't leave on her own." Carole was adamant in her statements and Cindi believed her. They continued their lunch in silence, both thinking their own thoughts on how lucky they both were.

Two months later, as Tony was cleaning up the kitchen, the telephone rang. "Hello?" He answered.

"Hello, Tony, how are you doing?"

"Fine Mrs. Fordham, how are you?"

"Tony, how many times do I have to tell you, call me Laura or Mother?" Laura's husky voice bubbled with laughter.

"I'm sorry, Laura," Tony chuckled." It's hard to believe you're my mother-in-law."

"It's hard to believe I'm going to be a grandmother." She laughed again. "How is school going?"

"Terrific. I just finished my second quarter and I'm hanging in there."

"I heard you made the dean's list again. Congratulations!"

"Thanks, Laura. I haven't started taking the tough courses yet."

"I have no doubt you will continue to do just as well. Speaking of doing well, how is our mother-to-be feeling?"

"She says she feels terrific, but I think she works too hard with her full time job and the house. She just laughs when I tell her to slow down. She's starting to show her pregnancy, so she's pretty excited."

"Is she available to come to the telephone?" Laura inquired.

"She's not here right now, Laura. She was going to stay late at work to finish a project. She called ten minutes ago to say she was on her way home. Shall I have her call you when she gets here?"

"That's not necessary tonight, Tony." Laura wondered silently for the hundredth time how her only daughter had ended up working at Danette's company. It was the only place that could bring back such painful memories. "I wanted to see if the two of you would mind if I came for a short visit this weekend? Why don't the two of you discuss it and call me later in the week."

"Laura, there's nothing to discuss. We would love it if you would come for a visit and stay as long as you want. We have your room all ready for you." Tony liked Carole's mother very much and he knew Carole would love to see her. "Carole will be so excited to see you. When do you arrive?" Tony's voice expressed his affection for Laura.

"I thought about arriving early Friday afternoon and I would leave Tuesday morning, if that's convenient.

"It's perfect! What's your flight number and when do I pick you up?" Tony asked.

"Oh Tony, I can't wait to see my mother, it's been so long." Carole fidgeted in front of him as they waited at the airport gate for her arrival.

"Honey, she should be here any minute. Her plane is at the gate." Tony couldn't help but smile. He would do anything to keep Carole as happy as she was at this moment.

"There she is, Tony!" Carole squealed as she darted toward the gate. Laura could just be seen walking through the doorway. Tony waited for several minutes as mother and daughter embraced. He wanted to allow them to have some time alone.

"Tony, don't you look wonderful!" Laura remarked, as she hugged him in greeting.

"Hello, Laura, welcome to Seattle."

"Thanks, Tony, it's terrific to be here." As Laura spoke, she gazed around the airport. Sadness settled over her face.

"Laura, are you okay?" Tony asked with concern.

"I'm fine, Tony. I was just remembering the last time I was in this airport," she responded softly.

Tony glanced at Carole to see if she had heard her mother's remark. She had. The look on Carole's face mirrored her mother's sadness. It broke Tony's heart to think of the cruelty that Laura had endured from her father. In an effort to cheer up Laura and Carole, he reminded them of the baby.

"Wait until you see how we fixed the baby's room, Laura," Tony enthusiastically remarked.

"Oh, Mother, Tony did a beautiful job. He found a cradle at a garage sale and stripped and repainted it. It's fantastic!" Tony's remark had done the trick. Carole was gushing with descriptions of the baby's room. Even Laura's face had a smile on it as the three of them walked through the airport.

Twenty minutes later, they were safely tucked into Tony's car and on their way with Laura's luggage and, as she put it, "a few small gifts for the two of them" in the trunk of the car. They all looked forward to a very pleasant evening.

"Carole, aren't you supposed to be at work?" Laura inquired. It was still early in the afternoon.

"My boss gave me the afternoon off, Mother. I told Denise that my mother was coming to visit and she told me that was reason enough to take the afternoon off. She's a wonderful person to work for." Before Carole could stop herself she began telling her mother about the company, oblivious of the affect she was having on Laura.

"Mother, the whole company is terrific! We have guidelines that everyone is of equal importance and we are! Cindi says it is because our founder, Dorothy Brennan, believed that way and taught Danette to believe in the value of her employees. We have a monthly meeting we all attend, and Danette talks to us about how the company is doing financially. She expects people to ask questions and give opinions. Mother, you would like her!"

At those words, Carole froze when she realized what she had blurted out. She sat silent in the front seat of the car, unable to continue. Tony had been watching Laura in the rearview mirror as Carole talked. At the mention of Dorothy Brennan's name, Laura's head had snapped up and her eyes had widened in surprise. At Carole's discussion of Danette, Laura's face had gotten very pale and she had turned her face toward the window. It was several moments before anyone spoke. Carole was clutching onto Tony's leg, afraid she had said something very wrong.

"It sounds like a wonderful place to work, Carole." Laura's normally husky voice was even more muffled. "I'm glad you are enjoying your job."

Tony glanced at Laura as she spoke. She was still facing the window, her face as white as a sheet. His heart went out to her. He loved Carole's mother. She was a loving and generous person. Knowing what her father might have done to her made him very, very angry. How could some one do that to their own child?

"Tony, why don't you tell my mother about your classes." Carole interrupted, gripping his leg even harder.

"Well, let's see. This quarter I took four classes, one in structural engineering, two architectural courses, and one drafting course."

"He got straight A's, Mother. They are talking about offering him a teaching assistant position next year," Carole boasted.

"That's wonderful Tony, congratulations. I have no doubt that you will graduate with honors." Laura was proud of her son-in-law. He had worked at night while going to New York University for four years and had managed to stay on the dean's list. He was hardworking, honest, and very good to Carole. He loved her to death and Carole loved him. Laura knew why. He was a very good and honorable man. He placed his family first and that meant more to Laura then anything.

"Thanks Laura. I love my classes. It's not work to me."

"No, he just studies every night until late and gets up early to study. He works so hard Mother." Carole responded, her love for Tony evident in her voice.

"Here we are." Tony remarked, as they pulled into the driveway of a darling little house, the gardens full of well-manicured flowers and plants.

"Isn't this beautiful," Laura remarked as she stepped out of the car.

"Wait until you see the inside, Mother." Carole raved as Tony unloaded the car. "It's close enough to school for Tony to ride his bike and it's only ten minutes to work by bus."

As Tony opened the front door and ushered them inside, Laura couldn't prevent the flood of memories that rushed through her. It wasn't over twenty years ago that she had gone to the University, it was yesterday that she and Danette had lived not far from this house. They had both pedaled bikes back and forth to class. Laura began to wonder if it had been wrong to suggest that Tony consider the University. Now Carole was working for Danette's company. It was so painful to listen to Carole even after all these years. Carole's voice broke through Laura's thoughts.

"Mother, would you like to rest for awhile?" Carole had noticed the strained look on her mother's face.

"I put your things in the spare room," Tony announced as he came down the stairs.

"No, I'm fine. Why don't the two of you show me your home?" Laura responded with a smile on her face. She needed to straighten up and forget the past. Carole and Tony proceeded to do just that, as they led her from room to room, with the baby's room last.

"Oh, Tony, what a beautiful cradle!" Laura exclaimed as she ran her hands over it. It had been set up in front of the window with a patch-work quilt tucked into it that matched the curtains. There were colorful animals all over them. The wallpaper also matched the quilt, and there were colorful animals along the base and ceiling of each wall. It was stunning. "The whole room is fantastic, you did a beautiful job!" Laura remarked as she continued to marvel over the room.

"We had a lot of help," Tony responded, grinning.

Carole shook her head in agreement. "Tony did the cradle, Denise, my boss, and I worked on the quilt and curtains, and Cindi and her girl-friend Susan helped us find and put up the wallpaper. Cindi's my best friend at work and she and Susan have been together for eight years. They even helped us with the painting and the carpet. They're wonder-ful." Carole rattled on, ignoring her mother's reaction.

"They all have been a great help," Tony agreed as he glared at Carole. She seemed to be going out of her way to remind her mother of the past. Laura's hand shook as she examined the quilt with her back to Tony and Carole.

"Well, you have all done a marvelous job. Now I think I'll take your suggestion and take a short rest before dinner, if we have time." Laura's voice betrayed her nervousness.

"Sure, Laura, dinner won't be ready until around seven. You have plenty of time to rest." Tony responded gently. "Come on, Carole, let's give your mother time to recuperate." He took Carole's arm and led her down the stairs as Laura entered the spare room and closed the door.

As they reached the bottom of the stairs, he turned to Carole. "What are you up to Carole? Can't you see the effect this visit is having on your mother?" Tony whispered with concern. "She didn't need to hear you discussing Danette and her company."

"Yes, she does, Tony. She needs to heal and let go of some of her pain," Carole responded adamantly.

"I know you love your mother, Carole, but don't you think you could slow down a little, just for her sake?" Tony pleaded quietly.

"Tony, you don't know my mother. She has always been able to deal with things head on. In fact, I am going to show her the photograph after dinner. It is the least I can do. I owe her happiness, and this is the only way I know how to help her find it." Carole was emphatic.

"Carole, what do you mean you owe her happiness?"

"She fought my grandfather for our happiness, and now I'm going to do the same for her."

"What can you do now? I agree you should talk to her about the past, but what else can you do?"

"I can reunite her with Danette." As Carole stated her remark, Tony's very rare temper exploded.

"Carole, I can't…"

"Tony, be quiet mother will hear you!"

"I can't believe you would plan such a thing, Carole. It has been over twenty years. Maybe your mother doesn't want to revisit the past. It is obviously very painful," Tony reasoned with his young, idealistic wife.

"Tony, I'm not that insensitive. I won't do anything my mother doesn't agree with." Carole reassured him with a kiss on his cheek.

A sigh of relief escaped Tony as he hugged his wife. There was only one problem with what Carole had said. When she set her mind on something she could convince anyone to go along with her. Tony knew Laura would not stand a chance against Carole. It had happened to him many times. He just hoped that Carole's plan did not cause Laura any more heartache. She had experienced enough.

"Let's go get dinner ready, Tony." Carole requested as she hugged him once more and headed for the kitchen. Tony watched her, and was reminded that his wife believed everything would turn out perfectly. It was one of the many reasons he had fallen in love with her. He would do anything to make it happen, but at this moment he was hoping his wife had not picked something that was impossible. It would break her heart.

"Tony, come on." Carole called from the kitchen. Tony grinned to himself. If anyone could reunite Laura and Danette, it would be Carole. He laughed outloud as he walked into the kitchen. Maybe he should warn Laura. She was in for quite an experience.

"Dinner was wonderful!" Laura remarked as the three of them sat at the dining room table.

"Thank you. Tony has taught me to cook many Italian meals. I was so rotten when we first moved here." Carole laughed.

"You weren't that bad, Carole." Tony chuckled as he also remembered their first few months of marriage.

"I was, too!" Carole responded giggling. "Mother, I couldn't even microwave correctly." Laura laughed with Tony and Carole as they told stories of Carole's cooking lessons.

"It took me several months to learn to cook when I was in college." Laura's eyes got a faraway look.

"How did you learn, Mother?" Carole inquired innocently, as Tony nudged her under the table.

"A friend taught me," Laura responded, with a smile on her face as she remembered Danette's cooking lessons.

"Listen, you ladies go in the other room and talk while I clean this up." Tony began to clear the table.

"Tony, let me help." Laura responded as she too began to pick up the remaining dishes.

"No, you both have some catching up to do." Tony replied as he took the dishes from Laura. "I insist." At that remark, he ushered Laura toward the living room. As Carole passed Tony, she reached up to hug him and whispered. "Thanks."

Tony hugged his tiny pregnant wife in response. "Good luck," He whispered back.

As Carole entered the room, Laura was gazing out of the front living room window. She seemed lost in thought.

"Mother, does this visit bring back lots of memories for you?" Carole asked gently.

"Yes, it does honey." Laura responded softly. "It was a long time ago."

"You never told me much about your time here." Carole remarked, hoping to get her to talk about it.

"Like I said Carole, it was a lifetime ago." Laura responded, her back still to Carole.

"Mother, I have something important to talk to you about." Carole spoke softly.

"Yes, honey, what is it?" Laura turned to Carole as she spoke. The serious look on Carole's face frightened her. "Are you okay?"

"Mother I'm fine, Tony's fine. This has nothing to do with us. I want to talk to you about you." Carol responded. "Please, come here and sit down." Carole patted the couch beside her.

"Honey, I'm fine." Laura answered, a puzzled look on her face as she sat next to Carole. "What's going on?"

"Mother, I want to show you something, and then you and I are going to talk."

Laura couldn't help but smile. Her beautiful daughter had always been so dramatic. Even when she was a tiny thing she had a flare for drama. "Okay, Carole, what do you want me to look at?"

As Laura watched her daughter, Carole reached out and handed a photograph to her. Laura took the photograph from her and gazed at it. Her breath caught in her throat as she saw who was in the picture. It was

Laura and Danette. Laura could remember exactly when it had been taken. They had gone out to dinner to celebrate moving into their house together, Michael and Peter had gone with them. It was Michael who took the picture as she and Danette stood in the middle of the living room. They had been so happy. They had looked forward to spending many years in the house.

"Where did you find this picture, Carole?" Laura asked as calmly as possible.

"I've had it for many years Mother, but that's not the point."

"What is the point, honey?" Laura asked softly, fearing the answer.

"This is Danette Johnson and you." Carole remarked, matter of factly.

"Yes, it is. We were roommates in college."

"Mother, she was more than your roommate."

Laura had been expecting the question since she saw the photograph. Taking a deep breath, she responded. "Yes we were, Carole. Danette was my best friend and my lover. She meant the world to me. We were together for over three years." Laura paused, waiting for her daughter's response.

"What I want to know is, why you left her and came home. I can tell from the photograph how much you loved each other." As Carole spoke, she reached out and clasped her mother's hands. "I know you, you wouldn't leave without good reason."

"Carole, it was a long time ago and it just didn't work out," Laura quietly explained. She unconsciously gripped Carole's hands.

"Mother, I love you very much but I know you're not telling me the whole truth. The one thing you taught me was true love is hard to find and once you find it, you were to hang on as tightly as possible. I know grandfather forced you to leave. Did he threaten Danette and her aunt? You would not have left for any other reason." Carole pleaded with Laura.

"How did you get to be such a smart daughter?" Laura responded, as her eyes welled with tears.

"I had a very good teacher." Carole smiled as her eyes also filled with tears. "I think you need to tell me the whole story."

"I would like to, Carole. I always planned to tell you. There just never seemed to be the right moment," Laura confessed, a slight smile on her face. "Danette and I met my very first day of college. My father allowed me to attend college at the University because I had applied and received a full scholarship. It wasn't the money. He just didn't think college was the place for me, especially pursuing an art degree. He refused to pay anything toward college." Laura paused in her story and Carole smiled with encouragement. Inside, she seethed with anger toward her grandfather.

With a deep breath, Laura continued. "From the first moment we met we were best friends. We remained friends until the first Christmas I went home. After spending a week away from her, I knew I had fallen in love with her. When I came back on New Year's Eve, I told her how I felt, and to my surprise and happiness Danette felt the same way."

"We were together for over three years. We lived in a small rental house not far from here and made plans to build our own home after we both graduated from college. We were scheduled to graduate in June of nineteen seventy-four, and Danette was going to work for her aunt. I was going to teach art at the University. Eventually, we planned to open an art gallery with our best friends Michael and Peter. In February of that year, I had a successful art show of my paintings. The only problem was Mother and Father came to town and attended the show. My cousin Devon thought he was being helpful and told them all about it."

As Laura continued to speak, Carole could tell she was reliving that evening. "As far as I could figure out, someone said something that my father overheard. He demanded that I have breakfast with he and Mother the next morning. That morning was the last time I saw Danette. Father threatened to call the University president and tell him about Danette. It was not acceptable to be gay back then, and he threatened to have her expelled. She was graduating with honors, and I couldn't let that happen to her. She had dreamed of graduating from the University ever since her parents were killed in a car accident. I would not allow anything to happen that would hurt her plans. Father also threatened to destroy her Aunt Dorothy's company if I didn't leave with Mother and him that morning. I knew he would do just that, so I had to leave. Danette was working, and my father took me to pack a few things and we left. I left a handwritten note for Danette. It was the hardest thing I have ever done."

Carole sat there quietly as Laura silently wept. Carole knew her mother needed to cry. She wrapped her arms around her mother as both mother and daughter mourned together.

After several moments, Carole began speaking. "I know grandfather forced you to marry my father. I'm sorry."

"Oh Carole, I'm not sorry. Your father was very good to me, and look at the treasure I received, you. I wouldn't change that for anything. I have been able to watch you grow up into a wonderful loving wife and soon-to-be mother. When your father married me, he made it clear all he wanted was a child. He also made several promises to me. He would let me live my own life quietly, as long as I acted the part of a loving wife. Your father and I respected each other very much. He also understood my need to paint. He allowed me to be me. I cared for your father very much, and I believe he cared as much for me. I know he loved you. He was so proud of you."

"I loved Father very much, Mother, but what about true love or passion? You always taught me to be honest with others and myself. Why didn't you get in touch with Danette and tell her the truth?"

Laura sighed as she responded. "She would have wanted me to come back, and I knew if I talked to her again I couldn't have said no to her. It was easier that way. She would be angry with me for a long time, but she would eventually heal and find someone else who would love her like she deserved. She was a wonderful person."

"With all that happened to you and Danette here in Seattle, why did you encourage Tony and I to come to here?"

"I knew you needed to get away from your grandfather. You and Tony needed to start your new family on your own. I also knew Tony would find the engineering school one of the best."

"Mother, I think there might have been another reason." Carole spoke quietly. "It gave you a reason to come back to Seattle." Laura remained silent.

"I have a story of total love and commitment that I would like to tell you."

As Laura listened to her speak, Carole told Laura of Danette's abiding commitment to her over the years. When she got to the part about the scholarship, their house, and Carole's job, Laura was openly weeping again.

"That is just like Danette. She would make sure that my daughter and her new husband were taken care of." Laura's voice was hoarse with tears.

"Mother, she did it for you," Carole responded. "She never hated you, she loved you. According to Cindi, she has never really had a serious relationship since you left."

"Oh, Carole, it was over twenty years ago. We are both different people." Laura whispered. "Too many things have happened since then."

"You should at least go talk to her, explain what really happened." Carole pleaded.

"Honey, I know you mean well, but let's just leave the past in the past, please?" Laura's face looked strained as she made her request.

"Okay, Mother, but I would like to ask you one other favor." Carole asked gently. "Would you go with me tomorrow to Peter and Michael's art gallery? Cindi gave me the address."

"They really opened one?" Excitement could be heard in Laura's voice.

"Yes, and I understand Peter is quite famous for his sculptures." Carole smiled as she saw her mother's eyes light up. Carole knew Peter and Michael would both be at the gallery. She had called them the day she knew her mother was coming for a visit.

"He was very talented in college. I remember he did this fantastic sculpture of a woman for Danette's aunt. She put it in her office. It had long flowing hair and robes…"

"It's still there Mother, right in front of Danette's office door."

"It must have been so hard for Danette when Dorothy died. Michael sent me a card when she passed away. She was Danette's only family." Laura's face softened as she spoke. "Dorothy was someone to admire. She was intelligent, funny, beautiful, and most of all supportive of everyone. She would go out of her way to help anyone in need."

"She sounds an awful lot like Danette," Carole remarked with a smile.

"Yes, Danette would be just like her aunt." Laura smiled in response her eyes glistening with unshed tears. "Honey, I'd love to talk some more but I am very tired. Besides your poor husband is probably lonely. I think I'd like to go upstairs now."

"Mother, I love you." Carole hugged her tightly.

"Oh, Carole, I love you." Laura returned her hug. "And Carole, thank you."

"You're welcome."

As Laura headed up the stairs to her room, Tony poked his head out of the kitchen. "Can I come out now?" He asked quietly.

"Yes, please, Mother just went up to bed."

Tony sat beside Carole on the couch and took her hand in his. "How did it go?"

"It went well, Tony. She's still in love with Danette, I know she is." Carole was emphatic.

"Carole, honey, I know you're doing this for your mother, but you need to let it go now. You have talked to her about everything now let your mother be. She has had quite a shock tonight, sweetheart. Let her make her own decisions."

"I know you are right, Tony," Carole conceded as she snuggled up against him. "I just want my mother to be happy again. She deserves to be."

"I know you do, and you are right. Your mother does deserve to be happy," Tony agreed as he pulled Carole onto his lap. "I wish your mother as much happiness as we have."

"Tony, wouldn't that be perfect!" Carole responded as she wrapped her arms around him.

"Right now what would be perfect is if my beautiful wife would come to bed with her handsome husband."

"I think that can be arranged." Carole purred, as she kissed Tony passionately.

"Let's go to bed, honey." Tony led Carole up the stairs.

CHAPTER 15

"Good morning, Mother, have you been up long?" Carole walked in the kitchen to find Laura seated at the kitchen table.

"Long enough to go for a walk with Tony."

"Where is he?"

"He's in the backyard working in the garden. He has done a beautiful job. The gardens are wonderful," Laura remarked enthusiastically.

"You should see his plans for this house, he has such wonderful ideas. He forgets it is only temporary, but he putters around the backyard every weekend. He wants to turn the whole backyard into a formal Japanese garden by the time the baby arrives."

"Speaking of the baby, are you doing too much, working full time and taking care of this house?" Laura sounded concerned.

"Did Tony put you up to this, Mother? I feel fine. The doctor says I am in perfect shape and I should be able to work up until the birth. I am planning on going back to work as soon as possible afterwards. We have this wonderful daycare in our building and I can work flextime. Everything is perfect. Really I am fine. In fact, I don't think I've ever felt better." She wrapped her arms around Laura's neck and kissed her hello.

"Just take care of yourself, little lady." Laura grinned at her daughter.

"Mother, you haven't called me that in years!" Carole grinned back. It was her nickname when she was very small. It brought back many childhood memories.

"Do you remember how I used to play dress-up in your studio while you painted?" She laughed at the memory.

"I remember you used to put on one of my dresses, my shoes, jewelry, and makeup, and then march back and forth in front of me. You used to pretend you were at a party. You were so serious." Laura, too, laughed as she remembered. Laura and Carole reminisced over many old memories. They did a lot of giggling.

"What are you girls laughing about?" Tony inquired as he entered the kitchen, giving his wife a kiss, and grabbing a cup of coffee.

"Just memories, Tony," Laura responded, still smiling. "How is the garden coming?"

"Good, in fact I'm on my way to pick up some paving stones this morning. I thought I would stop by the grocery store and pick up a few things. Do you have a list, Carole?"

"Yes, honey, it's on the counter by the telephone." Carole pointed and smiled.

"I should be gone about an hour. I know you ladies have plans this afternoon." With a quick kiss for Carole, he was out the door.

"You married a nice man, Carole," Laura remarked, as she watched Tony leave.

"I know, Mother, I'm so lucky."

"I'd say you both are."

Carole shook her head in agreement. If she had her way, her mother would be just as happy. Carole had plans.

"Are you ready, Mother?" Carole asked. She and Laura were parked outside the "Second Avenue Gallery". Laura was getting up the nerve to see Peter and Michael after twenty years.

"Yes, I'm ready." Laura took a big deep breath and stepped out of the car. She smoothed her knit dress and sighed. Carole followed her mother into the gallery.

"Laura!" Peter exclaimed as she walked through the front doors. "I would have recognized you anywhere!" A tall handsome gray-haired man stood in the entryway.

"Peter." Laura's voice cracked as he wrapped his arms around her. She returned the hug with total abandon. Carole stood to the side, smiling.

"Oh, Peter, you haven't changed a bit," Laura vowed as they continued to hug.

"Sure, I haven't." He laughed, "You're the one who hasn't changed, doll. Just as beautiful as ever. Let me look at you, you look fantastic!"

"Peter, this is my daughter, Carole." Laura announced proudly. "Carole, this is Peter Rankin, one of my best friends from college."

"Carole, it's nice to meet you. Boy, Laura, she is gorgeous," Peter announced with a big smile.

"Thank you," Carole responded with a blush.

"And she blushes just like you do." Peter laughed.

"Peter, you did it! You opened your own gallery!" Laura exclaimed as she began to look around. "It's wonderful!"

"Thanks, I've had it for fifteen years. It is home." Peter spoke proudly.

"Is that my Laura?" A tall dark-haired man with a huge grin asked as he walked through the gallery doors.

"Michael?"

"Of course." As Michael reached Laura, he hugged her tightly. Not a word was said as they silently swayed back and forth. Carole could see tears sliding down Laura's cheeks.

"Don't cry, Laura," Michael whispered. "You came back."

"Oh, Michael, it's so wonderful to see you and Peter. It's like I never left." She whispered back.

"Is this your daughter, Laura?" Michael inquired as he noticed Carole standing behind her.

"Yes, this is Carole. Carole, this is Michael O'Connell."

"Hello, Michael, it's nice to finally meet you in person."

"Carole, thank you for calling. I wouldn't have missed seeing your mother for anything." He pledged as he shook her hand. "I understand congratulations are in order. You're going to make Laura a grandmother."

"Thank you." Carole grinned as Laura groaned.

"Can you believe it, guys? It just seems like yesterday we were Carole's age, and now this." Laura chuckled. "Looks like we have a lot to catch up on."

"Come on in the office and let's visit." Peter requested, smiling as he ushered them toward the back. As they all walked through the gallery, Laura's eye caught a graceful sculpture of a woman standing as if in prayer. She had long flowing hair and elegantly draped robes. Laura recognized the work as Peter's.

"Peter, you did this!" She exclaimed as she went over to get a better look at the sculpture. "Carole, come see this! Peter, it is unbelievable!"

"It is beautiful," Carole responded in awe. She had never seen such delicate work.

"He did that last year," Michael bragged. "It's the only one he hasn't sold."

"Peter, I'm so glad you still sculpt," Laura remarked. "You always were so talented!"

"So were you, doll. Do you still paint?" Peter inquired.

"I still dabble a little."

"Mother." Carole interrupted impatiently. "She still paints and she's as talented as ever. She just doesn't show anyone what she does."

"Carole." Laura admonished, as they entered the back office.

"Have a seat." Michael suggested, as they all sat on two couches facing each other. He held Laura's hand as they sat side by side, with Peter and Carole seated opposite them.

"Can I see your work?" Peter requested of Laura. "I haven't seen any of your paintings since the night of your show." Color flooded his face as he realized what he said. Laura's face had gone deathly pale.

"I am sorry, Laura," Peter softly apologized.

"Peter, don't apologize, it was the last time I saw you." Laura responded quietly. They all were silent, memories from that evening so long ago floating in their minds.

"Have you seen Danette?" Michael asked, tension in his voice.

"No, I haven't." Laura responded, looking away from Michael and Peter. "It wouldn't be fair after all these years. Why remind her of old memories? Besides, she probably wouldn't want to see me." Laura did not sound very convincing.

"You should call her and ask," Peter suggested.

"I don't know. I'm only going to be here until Tuesday morning."

"You don't have to leave Tuesday, Mother." Carole interrupted. "You could stay longer."

"Carole, honey, I have commitments back home."

"Nothing that important, Mother."

"Carole." Laura's voice carried a tone of impatience. "Michael, what are you doing now?" She inquired as she turned to him, smiling.

"I'm still working for the same company I was working for twenty years ago." He laughed.

"It was a small software company if I remember correctly."

"No longer a small one, I'm afraid."

"Don't let him kid you, it's one of the largest companies in the United States. It has made him a millionaire!" Peter revealed, a grin on his face.

"Is that true, Michael?" Laura asked grinning.

"Pretty much Laura. All that time and hard work paid off."

"You always were a hard worker. Do you remember how much Peter and I would tease you and Danette?"

"Yes, and I also remember how Danette and I would have to pry the two of you out of your studios. You and Peter would have stayed there for days if we hadn't," Michael retorted.

"You're right," Peter and Laura agreed, smiling at each other.

"We had such fun." Laura reminisced. "It's like it just happened yesterday."

"I have an idea. What if we all go out for dinner? Carole, her husband, you, and Michael and I?" Peter asked excitedly. "We can catch up with each other and also talk about the good old times."

"How about it, ladies? Are you up to a good time tonight?" Michael asked, as thrilled as Peter.

"It sounds wonderful, but why don't you just take Mother out? You don't need Tony and I along," Carole responded. "The three of you have so much to talk about."

"Honey, you and Tony are more than welcome. I would love the two of you to get to know Peter and Michael," Laura insisted.

"Well, let me call Tony and tell him to get cleaned up. About what time?"

"Let's see, how about Michael and I pick you all up at seven o'clock. That will give me time to finish up at the gallery and get some things taken care of. What do you think, Michael?"

"Sounds perfect."

"Then we'll leave the two of you now, and we'll see you at seven." Laura announced as she stood up. "I'm so glad I'm getting to spend some time with you both." She turned and hugged Michael and then Peter.

"We're awfully glad to see you, too," They both agreed.

"Here's our address and telephone number. It was nice meeting you both." Carole remarked with a smile.

"It was wonderful meeting you, Carole. Thanks again for calling us." Michael hugged her tightly. "You don't know what it means to us to see your mother again."

"Yes, Carole, thank you so much!" Peter hugged her also.

Michael and Peter followed Laura and Carole to the entrance, where they quickly hugged good-bye again, and Carole and Laura went to their parked car.

"Mother, they're both very nice." Carole spoke as she unlocked the car door.

"Yes, they are. They haven't changed a bit. It's hard to believe they have been together for twenty-five years!" Laura marveled.

"Twenty-five years?" Carole exclaimed. "That's wonderful."

"We were inseparable, the four of us. In fact, when Danette and I lived at the dormitory, the rest of the girls thought we were dating Michael and Peter. It was easier that way." Laura chuckled as she remembered. "We used to have slumber parties, the four of us. Peter would always wear the most outrageous pajamas! We would stay up and watch old movies, eat junk food, and laugh. Mostly we would laugh." She told Carole several more stories of "the four musketeers", as she called the group. It was obvious to Carole her mother had many happy memories to share.

"I am serious, Laura," Peter earnestly spoke. "I need a partner. The gallery is too busy for just me." Carole, Tony, Laura, Michael, and Peter were sharing the end of a wonderful dinner. There was plenty of laughter, memories, and a few tears. All five had enjoyed themselves immensely. Tony and Michael immediately launched into a discussion on engineering, while Carole, Laura, and Peter discussed many other subjects.

"Mother, what a great idea!" Carole agreed with Peter. "You would be good at it."

"It's what you dreamed of doing when you were in college." Peter reminded Laura.

"Peter, I live in New York, not Seattle! Besides, I don't know that much about art anymore. I've been away from the art community for too many years."

"I don't think you have forgotten what you learned. You always had a good eye for quality art and that's what I need," Peter argued. "You would enjoy it, also."

"Mother, you know you would," Carole agreed. "You could live with Tony and I. We would love to have you."

"Carole, honey, I couldn't live with you and Tony. You need to be alone." Carole grinned. Her mother was thinking about it.

"Laura, there is a condominium for lease in our building. You could live there." Michael remarked. "It's a beautiful two-bedroom unit two floors below ours. It has a great view of the Sound."

"Laura, Carole and I would love to have you stay with us," Tony remarked. "We have plenty of room."

"I'll share my studio with you." Peter pleaded. "In fact, I think the first thing we should do is have a show of your work. Carole said you have painted all these years. Twelve paintings ought to be enough. Say, in three weeks, we could re-introduce you to the art world."

"Peter, wait a minute, you can't be serious!" Laura exclaimed. "You haven't seen anything I've painted in the last twenty years!"

"If it's half as good as what you painted back then, it will be a hit!"

"It is fantastic, Peter," Carole chimed in. "I know you'll love her paintings!"

"So, when do we move you, Laura?" Michael interrupted. "It sounds to me like next week wouldn't be soon enough."

"I'm off all next week from school. I can help." Tony volunteered.

"Whoa guys, hold on, I can't move here." Laura stuttered, panic in her voice.

"Give us one good reason why not," Carole demanded.

"Well, I have commitments in New York, I have a home there…"Laura's voice trailed off.

"Can you get out of your commitments?" Michael asked.

"Yes, but…"

"Can you sell your house?" Peter inquired.

"Of course I could, but…."

"What's preventing you from doing it?" Tony asked quietly, as the others looked intently at Laura.

"It would be scary."

"Mother, we'll all be here to help." Carole reminded her.

"It would be fun." Laura grinned.

"When do we leave for New York?" Michael asked with a chuckle.

"What do you mean we?"

"You're going to need some help selling your house and packing. Two people are better than one."

"I'll call on the condominium tomorrow, in fact you can look at it tomorrow morning." Peter interrupted.

"Oh my God, am I really thinking of doing this? I had better fly out tomorrow evening."

"All right Laura!" Peter cheered.

"Congratulations, Mother." Carole beamed. Things couldn't be working out any better.

"Do you need me to go with you, Laura?" Tony asked. He was excited for her.

"Tony, you stay here and spend some time with Carole, but I will need your help next week, if that's okay?"

"Sure."

"Michael, are you sure you want to go with me?"

"I'm ready!" He replied with a grin.

"Peter, you and I need to discuss the finances of this partnership before we plan too much more." Laura spoke in all seriousness.

"Laura, I already told you, your presence is what I need, not your money." He responded, equally as solemn.

"Peter, I can't be a partner without putting in equal finances."

"I'll tell you what. You have your show in three weeks, we display fourteen paintings, and you let me hang them and price them. The gallery will get fifty percent and you will receive the balance. That will be your payment for equal partnership."

"But, Peter, no one knows who I am. You will be lucky if one sells."

"That's the deal, Laura," Peter stated. "My lawyer will draw up the papers on Monday and I will send them overnight for you to sign."

"I can't believe we are doing this. After all these years it will finally come true?" Laura had tears in her eyes.

"It's almost exactly what we planned twenty years ago." Michael reminded her.

"Almost." Laura, Michael, and Peter sat silently, remembering the dreams and plans the four of them had made so long ago.

"Peter, Michael, I want to be the one to tell Danette I'm moving here. She should hear it from me." Laura stated emphatically. "I don't want her to hear it from someone else. It wouldn't be fair."

They all agreed. Carole and Michael exchanged a quick grin. The final stage in Carole's plan was coming together. With Michael and Peter's help, it wouldn't be long before Laura and Danette would be reunited and then nature would take its course. Carole was so sure of the outcome, she rejoiced. After being separated for over twenty years Laura and Danette would be together where they belong.

"I think we need some champagne to celebrate," Tony suggested as they all agreed. It was a happy excited group that toasted to new beginnings.

CHAPTER 16

Exactly two weeks later, the five of them were together again. This time it was a moving party. Carole was unloading boxes of dishes in the kitchen, Laura was directing the movers with the large items, and Peter, Michael, and Tony were busy connecting the stereo and the television. Laura suspected it had more to do with a basketball game on television and less to do with getting it set up correctly.

"It's hard to believe I sold my house and moved in seven days," Laura marveled.

"It was providence that the couple who purchased the house wanted most of the furnishings," Carole remarked.

"Its kind of fun to start all over. You know, I never did get to furnish my own home. Your father had everything. I never really liked all those heavy antiques your father had."

"Mother, it is meant to be, with this place being available and the gallery," Carole explained.

"I think you're right, Carole. Things have fallen into place." Laura couldn't help but think this was where she was meant to live. Everything had gone like clockwork.

"Laura, where do you want these boxes?" Michael asked, standing in the hallway. "One of the boxes has a tag that says photos and the other says odds and ends."

"Those go in the back bedroom." She answered. Seeing Michael holding the boxes reminded her of the day she moved into the dormitory at college. It was the day she met Danette.

"That is the last of it, ma'am," One of the movers announced.

"Thank you."

"Yes, ma'am, you're welcome."

Laura looked around the condominium. It already started to look like home. Tony had even brought several houseplants over to enhance the place.

"Mother, all the kitchen things are unpacked and your china is in the hutch. All that is left is to make the beds." Carole informed her.

"Honey, I'll take care of that, you go sit down and rest. You need to take care of yourself and the baby."

"Mother, I'm fine." Carole grumbled. Between her husband and her mother, Carole was lucky that they let her participate at all. Even Peter and Michael were getting in on the act.

"I'll help her Carole, you sit." Peter volunteered. "Let's go partner."

As he and Laura finished the bedrooms, Tony and Michael sat down with Carole and took a break. They had all been up at the crack of dawn and it was close to dinnertime.

"Whew, that's it." Laura sighed as she and Peter found places to sit. "We are done." She announced.

"Not quite," Michael remarked with a grin. "Peter and I have a house-warming gift for you."

"Yes, stay seated and I'll get it," Peter directed. Stepping into the hall-way, he returned with a loosely wrapped object. It appeared to be fairly heavy. Peter placed the present on the floor in front of Laura and grinned. "Okay, you can open it."

"You guys have done enough for me, you didn't need to give me a housewarming gift."

"It's nothing."

"Actually, it's something we've had for many years and we wanted to give to you." Michael explained.

Laura pulled the wrapping slowly away from a small sculpture. It was one Laura remembered well. They had given it to Laura and Danette many years ago on New Year's Eve, Laura and Danette's third anniversary. It was of two women embracing. The sculpture was very sensuous and beautiful.

"Mother, it's wonderful. You can put it on your mantel over the fireplace." Carole rattled on unaware of her mother's reaction.

"That is beautiful." Tony agreed. He too was unaware of Laura's response.

Laura's face became very pale, as she looked first at the sculpture and then at Michael and Peter. "I don't understand. Where did you get this?"

"Danette didn't want to keep it after you left." Michael explained. "We've had it ever since. We just didn't have the heart to give it to anyone else. We thought you might want it." He and Peter watched her closely.

"Thank you," She replied hoarsely. "It's perfect." Laura's eyes filled with tears as she was reminded of the pain Danette must have felt.

Noticing her discomfort, Peter announced, "Okay, everyone up to our place for dinner."

As they all got up to leave, Michael gave Laura a quick hug. "You can't change the past, Laura, but you can make sure the present is what you want and need. Live your life honey, you've had your own share of pain."

"Thanks, Michael." Laura hugged him back.

"Danette." Cindi came over the intercom Monday morning. "You have a call on line two." Cindi's voice betrayed her nervousness.

"Okay, Cindi, who is it?" Danette inquired, before she picked up the phone.

"It's Laura Benson-Fordham," Cindi responded, her voice sounding muffled. Carole had told Cindi that morning what Laura's plans were and that she was going to contact Danette, but Cindi hadn't been expecting her to call so soon. "Danette, line two." Cindi reminded her. Danette had not spoken one word since Cindi announced that Laura was on the phone.

"Thanks, Cindi." Danette spoke quietly.

Cindi would love to see Danette's face at that moment. Danette knew that Laura had come to town to visit Carole but Cindi would give her right arm to see Danette's reaction when she heard that Laura had moved to Seattle. This was exciting news. Cindi had to call Carole and tell her.

"Hello Danette speaking."

There was a short pause before Laura responded. The sound of Danette's voice had made her heart jump. "Hello Danette, this is Laura Benson." Danette did not need to be told who it was the deep throaty voice of Laura's was distinct. She recognized it immediately.

"I heard you were in town visiting your daughter." Danette responded, very business-like.

"Yes, I am. Actually, Danette, I was wondering if you were available to see me today. It's been a long time and I would like to see you." Laura tried to keep her voice calm. She took a big deep breath as she waited for Danette to speak. Danette sounded so serious.

"It has been a long time," Danette responded. "Can you come into the office some time this morning?" Danette had to keep it someplace public. "You could see where Carole works at the same time. You know, she's quite talented." Danette was speaking in low measured tones but Laura could hear the tremors in her voice.

"I can be there in one hour. Is that suitable?" Laura knew that Danette intentionally wanted to meet her at the office.

"Yes. I will see you at ten o'clock then?" Danette replied.

"Yes, and, Danette, thank you for seeing me," Laura stated before she hung up.

Danette sat there in stunned silence. She had managed to hide her pain and anger after all these years, but now it all bubbled to the surface. What did Laura think, that she could just waltz into Danette's office like nothing happened? Well, she would not let Laura know how she felt. She would smile and get through it. Besides, it had been twenty years. She was over Laura a long time ago.

"Danette." Cindi's voice penetrated her fog of thoughts and she focused her attention on her.

"Danette, are you all right?" She inquired concern threaded her voice. "You're awfully pale." Cindi walked toward Danette, who was seated at her desk.

"I'm fine." Danette snapped, unaware that she ran her hand through her hair, a trait Danette did only when she was under a lot of stress.

Cindi, knowing it had something to do with Laura, sat down across from her. "Danette, I not only work for you, I'm your friend. What's wrong?" She asked softly.

"Laura's asked to meet with me. She's coming in one hour." Danette wailed. "Why now? I don't need to see her. Oh, Cindi, what am I going to do?" Danette pleaded.

"Danette, you're going to straighten yourself up and meet with her." Cindi spoke emphatically, looking Danette straight in the eye. "You will be the Danette I know, always in charge, professional, and friendly. She must want to make contact with you for a reason." Cindi felt guilty, knowing what Laura was coming to discuss with Danette.

Cindi's directness affected Danette as she sat upright and responded. "I just don't understand, after all these years. Why now? Maybe it is because Carole works here. Do I look all right? It has been twenty years for God's sake. I look like an old lady!"

"You do not, Danette, you look beautiful, as usual."

Cindi meant what she said. Danette turned heads when she walked into a room. Her naturally wavy blond hair was cut in a short wind-blown style that accentuated her large blue eyes. She was tall and still very slender and her natural coloring was a golden tan. She had on a crème colored business suit with a dusky blue handkerchief in the pocket of the jacket. Her skirt was slim fitting with a slit in the back. The outfit showed off her long legs to perfection. With matching blue shoes and earrings Danette looked exactly like what she was, a successful, beautiful, and talented owner of a very large company. The one thing that set Danette apart was her natural sex appeal. It wasn't something you could learn. She just had it and both men and women were affected by it.

"Why don't you take a break and wander through the building for a while." Cindi knew that visiting with the other employees always pleased Danette.

"Good idea, I think I will. I will be back around quarter to ten and Cindi, thanks.

"You're welcome, now scoot!" Cindi grinned at one of her very best friends. She just hoped she was doing the right thing.

Cindi couldn't wait to meet the famous Laura and forty five minutes later, she got her chance. Cindi saw Laura walking down the hall to her office. From fifty feet away, Cindi could see how beautiful she was. She was a lot smaller than Cindi had expected, no taller than five feet. Her dark brown hair was pulled back into a simple bun at the back of her neck. She was dressed in a silk pants outfit that had an oriental look to it. It was a soft lemon yellow with white and peach swirls on the fabric. She looked a lot like Carole but was smaller and darker. She must have created a lot of attention as she walked through the office. She looked like she just stepped out of a fashion magazine. As she got closer, Cindi was reminded of the picture she had seen of both Danette and Laura. They had made a beautiful couple then, one dark and tiny, the other tall, and blond. What a gorgeous couple they would make now. They had both aged very well. As Laura walked through the office door, she smiled. Cindi's stomach flipped. This woman had sex appeal, also.

"Hello, you must be Cindi?" She remarked as she reached Cindi's desk. "I'm Carole Capoletti's mother. I have heard so many nice things about you from Tony and Carole."

"Hi, it's nice to meet you." Cindi responded as she stood up to shake her hand. Even her voice was sexy. Poor Danette she would not stand a chance. "I have heard so heard many nice things about you, too," Cindi responded politely.

"I'm here to see Danette at ten. I know I'm a little early, but is she available?" Laura inquired still smiling.

"Yes, she's in her office. Let me tell her you're here." Cindi buzzed Danette on the intercom.

"Danette, Laura Benson-Fordham is here to see you." Cindi tried to keep the excitement out of her voice. After twenty years they were going to meet again! It was so romantic.

"Thank you, Cindi, I'll be right out."

As Danette's office opened, Cindi watched Laura's reaction. A big deep breath was the only indication that she was nervous. Her eyes widened as she saw Danette in the doorway.

"Laura come in, welcome back to Seattle." Danette spoke with all the control she could muster. "You look wonderful, you haven't changed a bit." She smiled as she spoke. "Have a seat." She indicated a chair in front of her desk.

"You look fantastic yourself, Danette, as slender as ever. Do you still forget to eat?" Laura responded with a grin. She wanted to try to act as naturally as possible.

"Only when I'm busy," Danette responded with a slight smile. She could not believe she was responding to Laura so calmly. "What brings you to my office?" Danette inquired, looking directly at Laura. She was not going to waste any time.

"First, I wanted to thank you for what you have done for my daughter and son-in-law. You have been extremely generous and I am grateful. I know what you have done to help them get started here. You went out of your way for Tony and Carole." Laura's face and voice had become serious, her eyes dark and watchful as she spoke.

Surprised that Laura knew about her involvement, Danette tried to brush it off. "It was nothing," she responded with a wave of her hand. "The Sheppard Corporation assists many young students while they are completing their degrees, and your daughter was not hired by myself but by Denise Johnson. You might remember her. She worked for Aunt Dorothy back then. In fact, she is grooming your daughter for her position. She is due to retire next year." Danette's voice was purely business. She might have been speaking to a board of directors except for the hand she ran through her hair as she talked. Laura knew Danette was very nervous.

"I remember Denise. How are her children?"

"Both of them have children of their own. One lives in San Diego and the other is still in Seattle. Both are doing very well," Danette reported. "Denise is very proud of them."

"Danette, about what you have done for my daughter and Tony, I know you own the house they are currently living in," Laura revealed.

"It's part of the scholarship." Danette informed her.

"What I was wondering is, if you would be willing to sell it?"

"Why, may I ask?" Danette wondered how Laura knew she owned it, and how much more she had figured out.

"I would like to purchase it for Tony and Carole. It's perfect for them and they love it."

"Why that house? You could buy them practically any house in Seattle." Danette knew how wealthy Laura was.

"Tony and Carole can afford this one. Tony would not take a home from me as a gift. If I purchase it and allow them to make payments, it would be theirs." Laura's voice had become huskier and more urgent. It was obviously very important to her.

"Why doesn't Carole use her inheritance?" Danette also knew that Carole had received a sizable sum.

"She and Tony have decided to use that money as a trust fund for the baby's education. They really would like to make it on their own. I think they are very responsible young people."

"Fine. A gentleman named John Booth will handle the sale. If you leave a number where you can be reached with Cindi, he will contact you immediately." Still, Danette was all business.

"There's something else I would like to talk to you about," Laura requested.

"Yes?" Danette remained aloof and calm.

"I have decided to move to Seattle and I wanted to tell you in person." Danette's breath caught in her chest as she listened to Laura. She remained silent as Laura continued. "I have become partners with Peter in the gallery, and this last week I moved here." Laura's words came out in a rush.

Danette was stunned. "I spoke to Michael last night. He didn't even mention a word."

Danette felt angered at Michael and Peter. They were her best friends and they had not even told her they had seen Laura. She felt betrayed. Her face showed her anger. "So, you are the bearer of the good news!" Danette bitterly spoke. "How long has this been planned?"

"Danette, it happened two weeks ago, very quickly. I asked Peter and Michael not to say anything. I wanted to tell you myself." Laura explained, understanding Danette's anger.

"Why you? Michael or Peter could have told me. After all these years, why you?" The pain that Danette had felt twenty years ago came back in a rush. Her voice cracked and she ran her hand through her hair, hurt evident on her face.

"Danette, I owed you an explanation," Laura offered, tears in her eyes at the sight of Danette's anguish.

"You don't owe me anything. You can live and work anywhere you choose." The words sounded angry and bitter as Danette tried to control her emotions.

"I need to explain why I left over twenty years ago." Laura pleaded softly.

"I don't want to hear your reasons." Danette lashed out. She stood up and turned her back to Laura. "It was twenty years ago, it's in the past. Let it go, please?" Danette's voice pleaded with Laura.

"Danette, I'm sorry for hurting you." Laura couldn't stop her tears as she spoke to the back of her.

"I'm sorry, too. Thank you for telling me. Now please leave. I have a lot of work to do."

Laura took one last look at the back of Danette, she wanted so much to walk over to her and hold her. She knew she still loved her after all these years. "Thank you for seeing me, Dani." Unaware that she called her Dani, tears continued to slide down Laura's cheeks. She was the only person who had used the nickname.

Danette though had heard it, and her heart released all of her pent of feelings as tears streamed from her eyes. "Laura?" She called quietly as Laura walked to the door.

"Yes?"

"Good luck with the gallery. I know it was your dream to own one with Peter."

"It wasn't the only dream I had." Laura responded staring at Danette before she opened the door to the office and left.

Cindi watched her leave the office. She had never seen anyone look so sad. Afraid for Danette, she slowly opened the door to her office. Danette obviously did not hear her come in, as she was standing with her back to the door looking out the window. Cindi could see her shoulders trembling, and heard her quiet sobbing. Cindi backed out of the office and shut the door. She would make sure Danette had her privacy. Cindi couldn't help but hurt for two people who were experiencing such sorrow and pain. She needed to talk to Carole. Something had to be done.

Several weeks later, something was done. Carole was convinced her mother was still in love with Danette, and she was also sure that Danette was still in love with Laura. Danette had been miserable ever since finding out Laura moved to town. She refused to speak to Michael and Peter about it and was still very angry with them. Laura, on the other hand, was working long hours in preparation for her show. She refused to speak to anyone about Danette. Everyone had tried to get her to talk but she would not relent. She just quietly prepared for the show, the strain of her emotions showing on her face.

Carole and Cindi had gone over every idea they could come up with in order to get the two of them in the same room together. Both Laura and Danette acted like they had broken hearts. They were both miserable, hence Cindi and Carole had decided to act. It was eight-thirty Thursday night when Carole rang the doorbell to Danette's home. She was going to take action.

"Carole?" Danette's face showed surprise. "Is everything okay?"

"Yes, everything is fine, but I need to talk to you. I'm sorry it's so late." Carole apologized. She hadn't wanted to talk to Danette at work.

"Come in, is there something wrong at work?" Danette inquired, concern in her voice. "Have a seat." She directed Carole to a couch.

As Carole stepped into the living room, she knew she was right. Danette was still in love with her mother. Three of her mother's paintings hung on the living room walls.

"I was right." She blurted out. "You do love my mother!"

"What?" Danette exclaimed, shock apparent on her face.

"Danette, I need to tell you some things about my mother and I want you to listen, please?" Carole pleaded with her.

Danette, stunned with Carole's outburst, agreed. She sat down and listened intently.

"You never knew why my mother left you and I am here to tell you why. You need to know why she walked away from you even though she was in love with you." Carole told her, from the beginning, the story of her grandfather. When she got to the part where her mother was forced to marry her father, Carole offered even more insight.

"I knew my mother didn't love my father. He was more than twice her age. He treated her with very well but I knew they didn't love each other. He knew Mother loved you and was forced to marry him. He also knew that when my mother painted she was happiest because this kept you alive in her heart. He had a studio set up for her, and she spent most of her time painting." As Carole spoke, Danette had begun to cry.

"I didn't know about you until I moved here with Tony and remembered the photographs mother had saved of the two of you. But I will never forget what she said to me when I told her I had fallen in love with Tony."

"She told me I was lucky to have fallen in love. It happens once in a lifetime. You need to treasure all the time you have with each other and never give up on it, no matter what happens. That love will always be there. It is truly a heavenly gift."

"I knew then that she had experienced true love and had never let it go. Danette, it was you she loved all these years. You can see it in her paintings. I know you love my mother, you wouldn't have watched over her for so many years. You wouldn't have taken such good care of Tony and I if you didn't love her."

"How do you know?" Danette was stunned. Cindi must have told her.

"It doesn't matter. What matters is you belong together."

"Carole, it was a long time ago, we both have changed so much. What makes you think it would work out now?" Danette asked.

"Because I know, Danette. Go see my mother's show. You will know. She painted for you."

"I don't know, Carole." Danette hesitated. "I can't promise you anything."

"Just think about what I said," Carole requested. "That's all I ask."

"I will, and Carole, thank you for telling me. You obviously love your mother very much."

"I do. She deserves to be happy and so do you. It was so unfair and I will do anything to make it right." Carole passionately reminded her. "Thank you for listening."

As Danette let Carole out the front door, she thought long and hard about what Carole had told her. She had a lot of thinking to do.

CHAPTER 17

"Laura, will you relax. Your paintings are wonderful! I know they are going to be a hit." Peter reassured her.

A total of fourteen of Laura's best works were hung in the main section of the gallery. The minute Peter had gotten a glimpse of them, he knew. It had taken Laura a little over a month to choose the right paintings. Her colors were even richer than he remembered, and her make-believe jungle of plants and flowers leaped off the canvas. Each painting oozed passion with each brush stroke. He and Michael agreed with Carole. Laura had expressed all her feelings for Danette in her paintings and they were explosive.

"Peter, do I look okay?" Laura asked, nervousness in her voice.

"You look beautiful, as always Laura. Carole and Tony are with Michael setting up the food table and everything else is done. Relax." Peter responded sincerely.

He was dressed in a black tuxedo with a black shirt and a white bow tie. Laura had on a midnight blue silk dress that literally flowed over her body. It shimmered as she walked, with a slit that went up her right leg. Her hair was pulled back into a French braid. She looked very much like she did at her first showing twenty some years ago. It made Peter's heart hurt to look at her. He was praying Danette would show up. She was still not speaking to Michael and Peter she was so angry and hurt.

People had begun arriving twenty minutes earlier, many from the art community, some were Carole's friends and coworkers, and even more friends of Peter and Michael's. The show was, as Peter had a predicted, going to be a huge success. Already, several paintings had been purchased at very respectable prices.

"Look at all the people!" Tony raved as he, Carole, and Michael looked around the gallery. "They all love the paintings."

"Why wouldn't they?" Carole responded. She was busily checking out the room carefully.

"Carole." Cindi and Susan had arrived for the show. "Has she shown up yet?" Cindi whispered.

"Not yet, but I know she will soon." Carole reassured Cindi. "Peter, where is Mother?" Carole inquired, as Peter wandered toward the group.

"She's in the back, getting more champagne glasses. She's so nervous I had to give her something to do," He replied with a grin.

"How's it going?" Susan asked. "Her paintings are wonderful, and there's already quite a crowd."

"She's a big hit. We've sold three of her works and on the way over I had another inquiry into the purchase of one more."

"I thought you had overpriced them." Tony remarked in awe.

"No, people will pay for quality, and Laura's works are the highest quality."

"Carole." Cindi hissed. "Look!" Cindi pointed to the entrance of the gallery. Standing just inside the door was Danette. She had a wrapped package in her hand, and was wearing a beautiful red suit. She made a very stunning picture as she intently looked at the first painting on display.

"She came!" Carole exclaimed." I knew she would! Is mother still in the back?"

"Yes," Tony replied, a little puzzled at his wife's reaction. Michael and Peter had noticed Danette and also exchanged grins. In fact, with Susan and Cindi grinning, Tony seemed to be the only one who didn't understand. "What's going on, guys?" He asked.

"That's Danette." Cindi responded pointing in her general direction.

"Oh," Tony replied staring at her.

"Tony, don't stare," Carole demanded. "I'm going to go tell her where Mother is." Before anyone could respond, Carole had left the group intent upon her goal.

Danette had been slowly walking from painting to painting as Carole approached.

"She's even better than she was twenty years ago," Danette commented. "Her paintings create a magical world."

"Yes, they do." Carole agreed.

"Where is she?" Danette asked quietly. "She turned and looked at Carole with a slight smile.

"She's in the office getting some more champagne glasses. The door's right there." Carole pointed, and Danette walked toward the back.

Carole watched her walk through the open door and shut it. It was now up to fate, Carole thought, and Carole already knew the outcome. She smiled to the group as she walked toward them.

"What did she say, Carole?" Cindi asked, all of them waiting for an answer.

"She wanted to know where mother was." She answered with a grin. "I think it's almost time for a toast, don't you?"

At that very moment Laura had her back to the office door, rummaging through boxes when she heard the door shut. "Peter, I can't find any more glasses." She stated as she continued to look.

"Can I help you look?" Danette offered. Laura immediately stopped what she was doing and turned around.

"Danette." It was all Laura could manage to say, surprise on her face.

Danette smiled as she spoke. "Your paintings are even better than your first show, Laura. This show is a huge success, just like your show twenty years ago." Danette began to walk slowly toward Laura, who still had not uttered a word.

"Something must have inspired you to paint so passionately." Danette's voice had lowered and she spoke her words slowly in a very sensuous way. It caused shivers to run down Laura's spine.

"I was very inspired," Laura responded with her deep throaty voice. She could see the affect of her response on Danette, as her eyes darkened to a deep blue. Laura would never forget her eyes. They got that dark blue when she and Laura had made love. A warm wave of passion flooded through Laura's body.

"You should have told me why you left me," Danette stated, still staring directly at Laura. They were standing a little over three feet from each other. "I would have understood."

"You would have asked me to stay." Laura countered. "And I wouldn't have been able to say no to you. It would have ruined you and Dorothy. I couldn't allow that."

"You could have given me the choice," Danette responded.

"You're right, I should have spoken directly to you, but I couldn't. I loved you so much. I did not want to take the chance that my father would hurt you and Dorothy. Please try to understand. I didn't think I had any choice." Laura's voice was barely above a whisper. This was the most important conversation of her life.

"My heart was broken when you left. You and I had made such plans."

"I'm so sorry, Danette. If I could have done it differently, I would."

"Could you say no to me now?" Danette asked, her words barely a whisper as she took a step toward Laura.

"I wouldn't want to." Laura whispered back, as she looked directly into Danette's eyes. She too, took a step closer. They were inches from one another staring directly into each other's eyes.

"I brought a present for you." Danette informed her with a soft smile on her face, as she handed the wrapped box to Laura.

"Thank you, may I open it now?" Laura asked returning the smile. She would always love the way Danette smiled. She had a soft, gentle look to her face when she smiled. Neither one of their voices had risen above a whisper. Their eyes locked on each other.

"Please." That was all Danette said, but that one word almost melted Laura. She wanted to touch Danette so badly her knees were shaking.

Laura's hands shook as she opened the package. She slid the wrapping open, and saw several drawings lying in the box. They looked very familiar. She glanced up at Danette who was still smiling and then took a closer look at the pages. "These are sketches of the house we designed," Laura exclaimed softly, as she slowly looked at each one. Memories came filtering back, her and Danette lying in bed talking about each other's ideas while Laura sketched them. They had planned their home for many hours.

"I can't believe you kept them." Laura sighed as she looked up at Danette, her eyes filling with tears.

"It's a good thing I did." Danette boasted. "How else would we get it built?" She volunteered with a big grin on her face.

"Oh, Dani." It was all Laura got out as she and Danette threw their arms around each other, tears running down both their cheeks. They hugged each other tightly, neither one willing to let go for one second.

"Laura, I never did stop loving you." Danette pledged as she hugged Laura tightly.

"I never stopped loving you." Laura promised, as she kissed Danette. Neither could stop crying.

"We need to talk, Laura." Danette gasped as she and Laura kissed again.

"I know we do. Can you stay until the show ends?" Laura would not let go of Danette.

"Yes. I wouldn't miss it." Danette hugged her tightly.

"Can we join you?" Michael asked from the doorway, grinning from ear to ear.

"How about if we join you," Danette responded with a big grin to Michael, as she took Laura's hand and walked to the open door. The three of them walked toward the rest of the assembled group.

"Have some champagne." Tony stated, handing both Laura and Danette a glass. "We have a lot to celebrate."

"Yes, we sure do." Laura responded, her heart full of happiness. She threaded her arm in Danette's and squeezed.

"To Laura and Danette." Carole toasted. She had tears in her eyes and a smile on her face.

"Here, here." Everyone joined in as Cindi poked Carole and whispered. "You did it!"

Carole just grinned back. She had never doubted that she would be successful.

"Carole, I love you," Tony whispered to her.

"I love you Tony," she replied. Carole looked at her mother. Laura was looking directly at her daughter. Laura grinned and winked, and Carole returned it with a wink of her own, and lifted her champagne glass in salute. Everything was perfect.

It was two hours later before Danette and Laura had a moment alone. "Danette, can you follow me home to my condominium? We can talk there." Laura asked standing next to her car.

"Of course I will, Laura. Congratulations, your show was a huge success." Danette smiled as she spoke.

"Danette, I could care less about the show right now," Laura responded, touching Danette's cheek with her fingers.

"I will be right behind you." Danette clasped Laura's fingers with her own.

It was twenty minutes before the two of them finally entered Laura's home. Both became extremely shy as they found themselves alone in her living room.

"Your place is beautiful, Laura. It's exactly what I would have expected your home to look like," Danette remarked as she wondered around.

"To tell you the truth Danette, this is the first time since you and I lived together that I have decorated my own home. It felt wonderful to be able to choose everything myself," Laura confided.

Danette didn't know how to take the remark. Maybe Laura liked being single and on her own. Had she made a mistake?

"Danette, would you please sit down so we can talk?" Laura sat down on the couch next to her. "I meant what I said earlier. I have always loved you. I thought my heart would break when I wrote my note to you. I didn't want to leave you." Tears began to slide down her face.

"Laura, don't cry." Danette wrapped her arms around her. "Everything is going to be all right, I promise." She hugged Laura tightly.

"Danette, we lost twenty years with each other." Laura continued to weep.

"Laura, look at me please." Danette whispered, lifting Laura's chin up. "It doesn't matter what happened before. I'm here now and I still love you."

"Oh, Danette, why would you still love me after all I have put you through?" Laura asked, her eyes heavy with tears.

"Because we are meant to be together." Danette slowly leaned toward Laura, as she tentatively kissed her, her lips softly touching Laura's. A sigh escaped Laura as she responded to Danette's kiss. She slid her arms around Danette's neck and returned the kiss. The kiss deepened, as their passion for each other exploded. Danette and Laura could not get enough of each other, as they kissed each other until they were breathless.

"Wow." Danette grinned as she caught her breath.

"Wow, is right." Laura smiled in return.

"I'm not sure where to go from here," Danette whispered.

"I'm not sure either, Danette. It's been so many years and I am so nervous."

"You know, you are just as beautiful now as you were the day I met you. I can't believe we are here together after all this time."

"Danette, I have something to show you. Please wait here. I'll be right back." Laura walked down her hallway to a bedroom. It was only a couple of minutes before she came back to Danette and held her hand out. "Do you remember this?" As Laura spoke, she slowly opened her hand to show a gold antique diamond ring in the palm of her hand.

"You still have your ring." Danette grinned as she fumbled with her necklace. "Look what I have." She pulled a gold chain out of from under her jacket to show a gold ring dangling from the center of it. It was the ring that Laura had made for her.

"You are wearing yours?" Laura's eyes again glistened with tears as she smiled back at Danette. "I couldn't be any happier than I am right now. I love you, and I am hoping you were serious when you showed me our house plans."

"I am serious, Laura. I want to spend the rest of my life with you," Danette vowed.

"Starting today, please." Laura pleaded with a smile as she slowly stood up, her hand in Danette's. Danette's heart pounded rapidly as she followed Laura down the hall.

"Danette, how do you feel about making love to a soon to be grandmother?" Laura grinned as she turned to Danette and started to unbutton Danette's jacket. Her eyes had become a deep chocolate brown.

"This soon to be grandmother is my partner for life," Danette responded grinning back. "I will make love with her for the rest of our lives."

"I like how you talk, Dani," Laura whispered as she slid Danette's jacket off her shoulders.

"I like how you look," Danette responded.

"I will love you forever, Laura." Danette slid her hands up Laura's back as she pulled her close. Their lips met as the two of them slowly sank onto the bed, their arms and legs entwined. Laura and Danette rapidly shed the rest of their clothes, as they touched each other with reverence. Twenty years fell away as their familiarity with each other became second nature. Their overwhelming need to love each other completely swept through the two of them, as they renewed their pledge to each other in the most perfect way. Danette kissed every inch of Laura's body and worshiped the woman she had loved her entire adult life. Laura in return expressed the passion she had been painting about for twenty years by loving every inch of Danette's body.

It did not matter that they had been separated for over twenty years. Their love for each other was as strong and as true as it had been when they first met. Danette had never forgotten how she felt when she made love with Laura. She had never been able to find that feeling with anyone else. It was perfect.

"Dani, I love you," Laura whispered as her body trembled with wave after wave as an orgasm spread through her body. She held tightly to Danette, her eyes locked with Danette's. Their fingers firmly meshed together.

"Laura, I love you," Danette pledged as she, too, shivered with pleasure. She had waited over twenty years to feel this way again.

It was several hours before Danette and Laura lay exhausted in each other's arms. It was happy exhaustion that overtook them as they drifted off to sleep, their bodies wrapped around each other. Both of them were unwilling to let go for a single moment.

"Hey, sleepyhead." Laura spoke softly as Danette's eyes fluttered open. Danette's hand reached out and softly stroked Laura's face. "It is you." She sighed. "I was afraid it was a dream." She smiled.

"I'm very real." Laura reassured her, as she snuggled against Danette and wrapped her arms around her neck. "Now, I need to ask you a very serious question."

Danette's heart leapt to her throat as she watched Laura carefully, afraid of what Laura might ask. "What question?" Danette's voice betrayed her fear.

"When are you going to marry me?" Laura's eyes sparkled as she smiled at Danette.

Danette relaxed as she responded, a warm feeling washing over her body. "How about today?" She smiled in return, pulling Laura tightly against her.

"That would be perfect!" Laura purred as she kissed Danette deeply.

"Do you think we could put it off for a couple of hours? I have something more pressing at the moment." Danette grinned as she pulled Laura on top of her.

"I think I can be persuaded to wait a couple of hours, as long as you convince me it's worthwhile."

"Oh, I think I can convince you." Danette reassured her as she demonstrated her powers of persuasion.

CHAPTER 18

True to her word, Danette did marry Laura, as three weeks later in the company of their family and friends they celebrated their love with a commitment ceremony. Standing in front of all of them, Laura and Danette exchanged their rings for the second time in their relationship, and spoke the words they had felt for each other for over twenty years.

"It has taken us many years to find each other again, and I want you to know that my love for you has been as strong and unchanged from the first moment I met you. You are my heart and soul, and I will love you forever. Nothing will ever be more important then our love." Danette pledged.

"My love for you has always been one of the few perfect things in my life. Thanks to my perfect daughter and her meddling ways, I can spend the rest of my life showing you each and every day what you mean to me. I left you once and I thought I would die. I will stay with you always. You are my passion and I will love you forever."

As Danette and Laura exchanged a kiss, there was not a dry eye in the room. Everyone agreed that this was the most romantic of days. Carole couldn't help grinning as she watched the happy event. Life had turned out perfect for everyone.

Three months later, as Carole held her newborn son in her arms, with Tony by her side, she spoke. "How are the grandmothers doing?"

Tony knew immediately who she was speaking about. He would call his parents later to give them the good news. It was the crowd in the waiting room that Carole was referring too.

"I'll go tell them in a minute." He promised as he kissed his wife. "I want to look at the two of you for a few more moments." A few tears slipped from his eyes as he gazed at them. Carole had been in labor for almost five hours before delivering a healthy baby boy. She was exhausted and so was Tony.

"I love you, Tony." Carole laid there, her face full of sleepiness, a satisfied smile on her face.

"I love you, Carole." He whispered back, smiling. "You get some rest now and I'll go tell everyone the news. I'll be back in a little bit."

"Okay, honey." Carole barely spoke as she snuggled the baby next to her. He was sound asleep.

Tony tiptoed out of the room, as he entered the waiting room, he looked at the assembled group. Michael and Peter were seated on one couch snoring. Susan and Cindi were in chairs beside them, also sleeping. On the couch across from Michael and Peter were Laura and Danette. Laura was asleep, her head resting in Danette's lap. Danette was the only person who was still awake. Considering it was after four o'clock in the morning, he was amazed she was still up.

"She had a boy!" He whispered, smiling. "An eight-pound six-ounce healthy boy. He and Carole are both doing fine."

"Congratulations, Tony." Danette replied with a big smile and a whisper. "What's his name?"

Tony grinned again. "We named him after Carole's two favorite people, Lauren Daniel Capoletti."

Danette could not prevent the tears that slipped from her eyes. "You look exhausted." Danette responded, smiling at the young man who so recently had become family.

"I am." He said, sitting in an empty chair. "But right now I just feel very lucky, unbelievably lucky. Life couldn't be more perfect." Tears had begun to trickle down Tony's face.

As Danette looked down at Laura asleep in her lap with her hand tucked against her cheek, she sighed. The ring they had exchanged six weeks earlier at their commitment ceremony sparkled on her finger. She and Laura were enjoying their life together very much. She had a lot to be thankful for and Danette had to agree with him.

"You're right Tony, life couldn't be more perfect." She stretched her hand out and grasped Tony's. "Life couldn't be more perfect."

About the Author

Jeanne is a forty seven year old woman born and raised in the Pacific Northwest where she currently lives with her partner in their home in Seattle. She has been writing on and off for over twenty years but this is her first published book soon to be followed up with others. She has no shortage of stories since she currently has six others in work. As you can tell she believes in stories with happy endings and hopes you enjoy them just as much.

Printed in the United States
58972LVS00007B/1-18